The Outbreak Chronicles

Book One

Survival Ties

Trisha Leazier

BODY COUNT
PRODUCTIONS, INC.

Library of Congress:
ISBN, print: 978-0-9967678-3-5
ISBN, e-book: 978-0-9967678-4-2
First Edition, 2016.

www.bodycountproductionsinc.com

DEDICATION

This book is dedicated to my Omi thank you for encouraging me to follow my dreams wherever they may lead. Also to my husband Bryce and daughter Kylie.

A special thank you to my mother-in-law Jacqui: Without you this book wouldn't exist. Thank you for showing me how to make this dream a reality.

ACKNOWLEDGEMENT

Edited By: Nas Dean

Cover Design By: Rogenna Brewer

Cover Photo By: Jessica Leazier

Beta Readers:

Sue Collins

Lance Smith

Joey Griffin

Prologue

Marie stood in the kitchen holding a manila envelope neatly labeled with the logo of an electrocardiogram leading into a tree of life. Clydework Research Industries logo.

"Well what does it say?" I asked her as she scanned the letter.

"To Mrs. Forde or whom it may concern,

Here at CRI we pride ourselves on striving for the impossible. Our teams of scientist and doctors have had a breakthrough around the issue of failing organs. Our team has developed a process where they clone a failing organ and grow a healthy replacement." Marie read.

She glanced up, locking gazes with our dad and pointed out a section to dad.

"The hope is that with this development we could eliminate the need for a donor waiting list. We could take cells from the organ in question and grow a healthy replica free of any flaws that the original had." Dad read.

1

"How far into testing are they?" asked Marie's husband, Carter Forde.

"If you'd wait a second, I'm getting there." Dad responded.

"Well?" Mom asked.

"So far we have only gotten through the stages of animal testing with results that are off the charts of even what our teams were expecting. The amount of success the teams have seen has resulted in the FDA giving approval for us to continue into the next stage of trials." Dad read.

"Dave?" Mom asked. Dad lowered the letter.

"They are starting human trials and I meet the requirements." Marie answered.

"They say they will be announcing what they have found after they get the results from the human trials." Dad said.

"They've sent letters to three hundred people and there's a number for me to call to make an appointment."

"Are you serious?" Carter asked. We had been waiting the better part of two years for a heart transplant to come through for her.

Marie smiled as she nodded.

Carter laughed as he picked her up and spun her around till she begged him to stop.

The hospital in our hometown called to inform Marie that Dr. Minnow had made an appointment for her.

"It's convenient that we can do the biopsy here." Dad said as we waited in the mint green waiting room.

"It's nice that transporting the cells to the clinic is an option." Carter said. He was tapping his foot.

"Stop tapping." Marie said as she pushed Carter's knee down, "You're making me nervous."

"Marie Forde?" A nurse in Felix the Cat scrubs called.

"That's me." Marie responded and stood up, "Is it okay if my husband comes in with me?"

"Of course, just make sure you do what the doctors tell you to." The nurse answered and led them out of the waiting room.

All we could do was stare at a muted TV while we waited for Marie and Carter. When my sister walked into the waiting room an hour and a half later I took in her appearance. Standing at five feet tall and barely weighing ninety-eight pounds, Marie had always been tiny. With her long blonde hair and big brown eyes she looked a lot younger than her thirty-two years. People who didn't know us sometimes thought she was my younger sister. Since her heart started to fail her two years ago, she looked even smaller to me.

At last the day arrived. Marie and Carter waited while we were loading up to take her to the clinic for the transplant.

I sat in the third row seats of the Tahoe watching Marie sleep. She was leaning on Carter in the seats in front of me and she looked so peaceful we could have been heading to go camping. Instead we were heading to CRI's clinic. We had just started to drive but I was already looking at the clock on the radio annoyed by the time.

"Do we have everything we need?" Mom asked.

"Yes Joyce." Dad answered.

"Is everyone comfortable?" Mom asked as she played with the temperature controls.

"Yes." Carter responded.

"Should we stop for breakfast?" Mom asked. She was spinning her wedding ring around her finger.

"Mom stop. It's going to be fine. Just relax." Marie said.

Mom finally settled for tuning on the country station Marie loved. We sat in the car watching the landscape go by heading towards Phoenix with the music drifting among us.

I must have fallen asleep because the next thing I knew Carter was shaking my shoulder.

"We're here Ash." He said, as my eyes opened. It was bright and I had to blink a few times to clear the blue tint sleep had left on my vision.

Above the entrance, the facilities' name stood in red letters on a lined white background. I could see Marie's hand shaking as she walked in front of me holding tight to Carter. She had always hated hospitals of any sort. I walked up beside her and snatched the shaking hand, squeezing it to comfort her.

"Is this a medical research center or a theater?" Carter asked and pointed to the letters.

Marie didn't respond, but she did a nervous hiccup giggle as she shook her head.

Dr. Minnow was talking to the receptionist as we walked into the lobby. He smiled at us and started towards us. He was fairly tall, standing at about six feet and he had dark brown hair that was peppered through with grey. His dark brown eyes were almost black in color behind black-rimmed glasses. He wasn't extraordinary to look at; his face had average features that would easily be lost in a crowd. In fact the only thing that etched his face into my mind was the simple fact that he was Marie's doctor. He was going to be doing the procedure.

"How was the drive down?" He asked as he stopped in front of Marie.

"Long." Dad answered with a little nervous chuckle.

"Well we are all ready to get the prep work out of the way and get you in and out of surgery Marie." Dr. Minnow said, getting right to the root as to why we were here.

"Okay, I'm ready." Marie answered so quietly it was almost a whisper of sound.

Dr. Minnow led Marie and Carter down the hall away from us. Carter returned a short while later to wait the four-hours with us till Marie would enter into the recovery ward.

I was making my five hundred and thirty third lap of pacing the waiting room when Dr. Minnow finally came out. We all stood, anxious to hear how Marie was.

"Marie is in recovery now and everything went as we had hoped. No complications at all and the nurse will come get you when she wakes up so you can visit her." He informed us, "Of course she will be staying for the next few days. The paperwork included her husband staying as well. Have the rest of you made arrangements nearby?"

"Yes we have." Dad answered quickly.

"Good, replacing a heart is never easy, so Marie will need a lot of rest to ensure she heals well." Dr. Minnow told us as he looked at his chart. Without saying another word to us he turned and headed back from where he'd come.

"Anyone want coffee or a candy bar?" Mom asked for the tenth time since Dr. Minnow had left us.

"Joyce, honey, please stop asking us that." Dad told her for the fourth time.

I avoided looking up at the clock; it was intentionally mocking me with the slow ticking noise. I was almost jumping out of my seat every time the doors opened and someone walked by us. I was about to give in and look at the stupid clock when Carter came through the doors and waved us over to him. We followed him to Marie's room where she was laying in the hospital bed her head on a pile of pillows.

"Hi sweetheart, how are you feeling?" Mom asked as she grabbed Marie's hand.

"I feel groggy, Mom." Marie answered as mom patted her hand.

We sat there with her until the nurse came in to tell us that visiting hours were over. We could come back the next morning at eight.

Dad, mom, and I hugged Carter and Marie before we headed out. We went to the Days Inn where we were going to stay for the next few days.

"She looked well. Didn't she look well, Dave?" Mom asked dad as we entered our room.

"Yes Joyce, she looked as well as can be expected after a surgery like that. Now let's get some rest so we can be cheery for her tomorrow." Dad responded, kissing mom on the cheek.

The following days were a blur of hospital visits. We watched Marie get stronger than we had seen her since she was diagnosed. When were in the hotel room, crappy TV movies played as constant background noise.

"I'm happy to say that Marie is well enough to travel back home." Dr. Minnow stopped to tell us the third day while we were with Marie.

"Are you sure? It seems like we just got here." Mom said.

"I'm sure, I know it seems quick but her vitals are good and she meets all the requirements to continue healing at home." Dr. Minnow said.

"Thank you Doc." Dad said and reached his hand out to shake Dr. Minnow's.

"I know the drive back to Flagstaff will take about two hours and Marie will be mildly sedated for that." Dr. Minnow explained.

"What do we need to do when we're home?" Carter asked.

"Monitor her; make sure she takes her medications at the same time each day. She'll get tired quickly while she's still healing and her appetite may vary from day to day." Dr. Minnow answered as he handed Carter a pamphlet.

"Anything else?" Dad asked.

"If you are worried about anything or unsure if its normal just give us a call and we'll talk you through it." Dr. Minnow answered, "Have a safe trip home."

"Thank you again Doc." Dad said.

The nurses already had Marie packed for the trip home by the time we got to her room.

Chapter One

One month later

My best friend, Sawyer, sat on the counter swinging her legs as she watched the pancakes cook. Her green eyes were hidden behind cat eye contacts. Her clothes were simple, a black T-shirt and torn up jeans and her black converse tennis shoes. She had a cat ear head band on to go with her eyes. The garbage truck was rumbling outside as it stopped to pick up the trash.

The TV in the living room was muted but the news station was showing images from some sort of riot. There were people with injuries. The suspect was restrained in a strait jacket before they went back to the anchors with their perky smiles.

"Are you seeing this?" I asked pointing the spatula towards the TV.

"Yeah almost every day lately with the same things." She answered, "I don't get how the anchors can smile after showing those clips."

"I don't either. I've avoided most of the news lately."

"Not missing much. Same stories about a shooting here or a riot there, lately more riots though." Sawyer said, "Hey start flipping or they'll burn."

"What?" I asked, "Oh." I cringed when one of the four pancakes revealed that it had burned, hitting my nose with the smell.

"So Marie seemed way more energetic last night." She said as she flipped the three good pancakes onto Marie's favorite mint green plate.

"Yeah still healing and recovering so yesterday was one of the better ones." I agreed.

Luckily for Sawyer's hair I thought to myself.

"I still can't believe you actually talked her into not only cutting your hair but adding blue and pink highlights. Your mom is going to be pissed."

"I could say I got attacked by angry highlighters." Sawyer said as she shrugged and twirled some of her now chin length platinum blonde hair with her finger.

I rolled my eyes causing Sawyer to start laughing as we finished making breakfast. Marie staggered in followed closely by Carter.

Her brown eyes were glazed over and she was drooling.

"Morning." I greeted her as she stared at me.

She didn't say anything.

Then she growled.

I stepped back coming up against Sawyer's legs.

"Hon, the girls made you breakfast." Carter told her calmly as he touched her shoulder.

She snapped at him like a dog would. Carter didn't flinch as he stepped to put himself between Marie and us.

"Marie." He said and clapped his hands in front of her face.

She shook her head at the sudden noise.

"What?" she asked, "Oh, you made my favorite."

Marie took the plate I was holding and went into the dining room. It was quiet for a moment while we all took in what had just happened.

"What was that about?" Sawyer asked, breaking the silence as she slid off the counter.

"I don't know; she's had a couple mornings like this. She's just a little off I guess from the medications." Carter responded.

"You call that 'a little' off?" I asked, "Carter, she growled at us."

"She doesn't seem to remember the spells after she snaps out of them. I'm going to call Dr. Minnow after breakfast." He said.

We heard glass shatter in the dining room.

"Marie, are you okay?" Carter called.

There was no answer.

Carter took a step towards the doorway when she came in. Her bare feet bled from where she had stepped on broken glass. She didn't seem to notice anything around her.

"Marie?" I asked, stepping towards her.

She looked at me; her eyes blank as she started screaming and lunged.

Carter stepped quickly behind her, wrapping his arms around her shoulders before she could reach me. He pulled her into his chest.

She kept screaming as she clawed at his arm. She bit him taking a chunk of flesh from his arm. Carter grunted but held on as she flailed around trying to get free. Blood was dripping from her chin onto Carter's arm. It joined the blood spilling from the bite down her white shirt.

Sawyer and I stood frozen as Marie continued to scream. Neither of us even turned towards the sound of the door opening.

The neighbor, Sam, walked in.

Marie didn't even glance at him. Her gaze was locked on me.

An explosion echoed through the room followed by an acrid and sour smell.

I finally turned my head and looked at Sam to see him holding the revolver he always carried on his hip. Marie slumped into Carter. A hole seeped blood from her chest. Her new heart pumping as the screaming faded to a gurgle. Carter lowered her to the ground and placed both his hands over the wound using his body to put pressure there.

"What the hell?" he yelled at Sam.

"She was crazed." Sam told him. "Same thing happened to the Nathan's down the way."

"She wasn't crazed; she was having a reaction to medication." Carter responded.

Sam took off his cowboy hat showing his short cut black hair streaked with grey. He placed the hat on the counter. My gaze stayed glued to Marie; she stared back.

I dropped down to the tiles.

She was dead and no one could explain what had just happened.

"We need to call 911." I said, still staring at Marie.

"Y-yeah I-I can do that." Sawyer stuttered.

"What are you talking about?" Carter snapped at Sam as he continued to hold on to Marie like he could bring her back.

"You know Vick and Jenny Nathan down the street in the brown house? Their boy Josh had his lungs replaced a month ago just like Marie's heart." Sam told us, leaning against the counter rubbing his eyes. "He started acting weird and yesterday went after Jenny in the kitchen, bit Vick in the process. When he got to Jenny he walked right into the knife she was holding from making dinner, didn't even noticed it. Vick pulled him away before he could do anything to poor Jenny and he died."

"Wait. What?" Sawyer asked from behind me. She had dated Josh for two years before he got sick and broke it off.

"Police were there and everything. They took the body to the morgue and so far I haven't heard anything else." Sam told us. "Vick seemed okay, had a good piece taken from his shoulder though. They bandaged him up there and let him stay at home."

"Josh had a transplant like Marie?" Sawyer asked. She seemed pretty lost in her thoughts. She was not processing much. After everything with Marie and then finding out the boy she still loved was killed.

"Yeah from that Clydework place, signed up to be a human trial." Sam answered.

I heard Sawyer fumble her phone out of her pocket. Before she dialed anything, I watched Marie's open brown eyes bleed into red.

"What's happening to her eyes?" I asked.

"What?" Carter asked.

"Her eyes." I said again.

Carter looked down and studied her eyes as I heard Sawyer telling the 911 operator what had happened.

"It could just be some reaction from the medication she was on." Carter answered.

Sawyer was repeating herself to the operator.

Marie's hand twitched sending a flutter of hope through me. She blinked but she didn't draw in a breath.

A low growling drew Sam's attention to her. Carter was leaning towards her when she rolled into a crouched position causing him to jump back.

Her red glare was glued to Sam and her teeth were bared.

Carter froze.

"Marie? Sweetie helps on the way. I think you should lie down until the paramedics get here." Carter said to her. His hands were shaking as he raised them towards her. Her head snapped to him for a minute and she hissed.

"What the—" Carter said.

"Carter, step back slowly." Sam interrupted.

The sound of his voice snapped Marie's attention back to him.

Marie tilted her head from side to side as she growled at Sam.

"Marie, please calm down." Carter tried again to reason with her.

"Carter, no." Sam snapped before he could move towards her.

Marie whipped her head back and forth between Sam and Carter until her gaze stopped on Sam.

She lunged at him.

The second shot from the revolver echoed in the kitchen as they fell to the tiles.

He rolled her off him showing the hole in her forehead that wasn't bleeding.

Sawyer screamed and dropped her phone.

I could only stare at Marie in shock.

I barely registered the operator in the background from Sawyer's phone, faintly telling us help was on the way.

Like they would be able to help with what had just happened.

Chapter Two

I was staring out the window as the garbage truck made its weekly rounds again. I turned when I heard something shatter in the kitchen.

"You okay?" I asked when I found Carter staring into the sink.

"Yeah, just lost grip on my damn cup." He answered and I could see the black mug sitting in pieces, some still held a few drops of coffee.

"I'll clean it up when we get back." I told him as I squeezed his arm.

"I'll do it don't worry." He said, "We have to go."

We were heading to Marie's favorite park where Carter had decided to have a celebration of life for her. We couldn't have a real funeral yet. Clydework had sent people over to gather Marie's body to run tests on and see if they could figure out what had happened.

So far the only comments they had given us was that she must have mixed medications that caused her reaction.

No charges were pressed on Sam. The police never even handcuffed him since it was self-defense. He probably saved our lives.

The Nathans' came to the celebration. Vick still had a bandage on his shoulder; you could see the corner of it peeking out of the neck of his shirt. He didn't look well, his olive skin had no real color to it and he seemed to be leaning on Jenny as he coughed violently. Jenny looked as if she hadn't slept for days. Her blue eyes were swollen from crying. She looked like she was carrying the weight of the world on her shoulders, and it was crushing her.

I threw the white rose petals I was holding into the air to mix with the others floating on the breeze to symbolize Marie leaving us.

Then Vick started coughing again.

His fit sent him to all fours, blood and saliva spraying onto the ground.

Jenny was trying to help him up when he turned on her.

He ripped a bite out of the curve of her neck before anyone could get to them.

Sam appeared from out of nowhere and pulled Vick off Jenny while people panicked.

Vick went after a few different people, biting anyone who grabbed him. Jenny was crying holding whatever piece of cloth Sam had given her to the bite. She stared after her husband as he disappeared down the street. Sam helped us load her into Carter's Tahoe and jumped in.

"We should take her with us to your house." Sam told Carter. Nothing seemed to faze Sam; he processed what was happening around him and reacted.

"You're probably right." Carter agreed as he jumped in and started the Tahoe.

"Jenny, we are taking you back to the Forde's home in case Vick goes back to your house." Sam told Jenny, even though she looked like she wasn't hearing anything.

Carter sat with the SUV running as he stared out the windshield. There were a few people helping bandage wounds on others but more were trying to get back to their own vehicles.

One man started pounding on Carter's window.

He looked like he had been out for a run and still had his headphones in.

Carter put the SUV in drive and slowly moved away from the man.

I watched out of the back window as he ran to a pickup truck and jumped into the bed. The driver took off so fast the runner stumbled and flipped back onto the pavement. Before he could move a red car backed over him, the driver didn't even stop to see what they had ran over. No one said anything as we drove away from the park.

I kept thinking we never finished Marie's celebration.

Jenny was quiet the whole drive to the house. I found myself wondering what was going to happen with her husband since he was still out there.

I noticed Carter was sweating even with the A/C on. He was trying to do too much and I was sure he was making himself sick.

I tried not to look out the windows. Nothing made sense. The image of the runner falling was seared into my brain and kept replaying.

"Everything is going to be okay. Everything is going to be okay." Carter kept saying. I wasn't sure if he was talking to any of us or himself.

Jenny's soft whimpers drew my attention back to her.

Her dark skin was chalky and pale making the blood dripping from the bite look obscene.

There was more chaos outside the hospital as we ended up in a standstill. Traffic was barely moving. People were screaming and running. No one was looking where they were going.

My heart pounded as I watched a woman in a torn yellow sundress slapping her hands on the driver window of a black Mustang.

Another woman climbed onto the mustang and lunged at the yellow sundress woman.

Tha-thump. Tha-thump.

The door to the Mustang opened. A man in Aviator shades pulled the woman in the sundress into his car.

Tha-thump. Tha-thump.

The other woman clawed her way on to the back of the car as it drove away.

We rolled closer to the hospital entrance, there was a nurse on the ground, not moving, a man pinning her. As we drew closer he looked up, we were close enough to see his eyes glowing red, and he was taking huge bites from the nurse's body. Half her face was down to bone, even the eyeball gone. I couldn't tell where her red hair ended or where the bloody mess started. Her remaining eye was open and blinking, glowing red as she started to shove out from under the man. He no longer had interest in her as he let her go.

I saw Jenny look out the window. She stared at the man and started to cry and crawl over me clawing for the door handle.

"What are you doing?" Carter snapped from the front, seeing the movement in the rearview mirror.

"That's Josh. He's not dead." She screamed.

Josh watched the car with a blank stare until one of the panicked people ran in front of him. Josh launched himself at the man catching his leg as he fell and biting into the man's calf. The man kicked Josh in the shoulder with his free leg. He was up and running before Josh recovered.

Sawyer grabbed Jenny and shoved her back into her seat.

"It's not him." She snapped when Jenny tried for the door again.

I wondered what it cost Sawyer to say that as Jenny stopped fighting her and stared out the window at what had been her son.

Sawyer had tears running down her face freely by the time we pulled up to the house. I climbed out of the Tahoe as Carter started to cough.

Sawyer and Sam helped Jenny into the house. I went to open the driver door to help

Carter. As I grabbed the handle he looked up at me through the glass.

His lips were pulled back from his teeth in a snarl and his eyes were glazed over.

I was already backing away when he started clawing at the window and throwing his body against the door.

I turned and ran the few yards to the house, slamming the door as I heard glass breaking behind me. I locked the dead bolt and waited to hear him pounding on the door.

But the noise never came.

Sawyer came around the corner and saw me.

"What's going on? Where's Carter?" she asked me.

"In the car. I think he may be out now." I told her as I fought to catch my breath.

She followed me to the window and looked out.

Carter was dragging himself out from the shattered window of the driver's door. He didn't even glance at the blood coming from where the glass was cutting into his flesh.

"What's going on?" Sawyer repeated, stepping away from the window and bumping right into Sam.

"I don't know." I told her as I looked at Sam for answers.

He squeezed Sawyer's shoulder and shook his head.

Jenny was asleep on the couch when Sam slipped into the back yard. He started bringing in lumber Carter had got to build the deck Marie had wanted.

"I think we should board up the windows." He told us.

"Do you think that will keep them out?" I asked.

"It'll be better than just glass." He answered.

"Carter was planning to put up shelves. I can show you where he had all of it." I said.

"Lead the way." Sam said.

"Do you need help?" Sawyer asked him.

"Sure. You can come and help us get everything in here." He told her. I realized he was giving her a task to keep her focused and busy.

I led Sam and Sawyer to the garage where Carter had piles of pine wood he had been in the process of staining to the color he wanted.

Sam grabbed a whole pile and went back to the front entrance. Sawyer and I split the next one. It took a few trips before all the wood was in the house. Off to the side there were two five gallon buckets of long nails. But we only found two hammers

"Will this be enough?" I asked when we had everything together.

"We'll work through what we have and if we run out we'll tear apart wood furniture to use."

Sam had Sawyer hold up the planks of wood as he nailed them into the wall on one side and I did the other.

It felt like every time a hammer hit one of the nails the sound echoed through the house.

My ears were ringing with the banging by the time we got to the last window.

With the windows boarded up and everything quiet again, Sam gathered Sawyer and me into the dining room.

He looked pretty serious as he sat down and waited for us to take seats.

"Ashlyn, can you find me some paper and a pen please." Sam asked me after a moment.

I went to the kitchen and grabbed the notepad and pen from by the phone.

"Well from what we've seen, it appears we have at least two stages of whatever is happening." Sam told us as he tapped the pen on the table.

He labeled the columns 'stage one' and 'stage two'.

"Stage one: we've got people going crazy and attacking others." He said as he wrote.

Both Sawyer and I watched him.

"Stage two: we've got people with their eyes turning red, should be dead, and still attacking others." He continued, "It seems like everyone infected hit that stage one part. Except for that nurse outside the hospital."

"How does that help with anything?" I asked.

"I'm just using a common survival technique, we use our observations of the situation we are in and to the best of our abilities figure out what's going on around us and how to survive." Sam answered.

"So what do stages mean?" Sawyer asked.

"First we need to figure out what everyone has in common." Sam responded, "Ashlyn, what did Marie and Josh have in common?"

"They both got transplants from Clydework about a month ago." I answered, wondering why he was asking me something he already knew.

"Okay, Sawyer what do Vick and Carter have in common?" he continued.

"They were both bit about eight days ago." She answered, "But you already know that."

"Yes I do. We know Josh died, like Marie did, but I was here and we saw her die again. Where was Josh?" he asked.

"He was at the hospital, in the morgue and he must have come back like Marie did." I answered.

"Yeah they must have pulled him out for the autopsy only to find a...zombie." Sawyer responded struggling on the word 'zombie'.

"It appears so. We saw Josh eating that nurse and she came back with red eyes like Josh and Marie had. It would seem that stage one can be skipped if the victim dies with no damage being done to their brain." Sam said, pointing out the facts. I had never realized before just how smart he really was.

"So what does all this mean?" Sawyer asked as she fidgeted in her seat.

"It means we have two dangers out there to face. We have our stage one crazed people and our stage two red eye people." Sam responded "And we know we could have days before anyone bit turns crazed."

"Are you saying I have only days before I go crazy like Josh and Vick did?" Jenny interrupted as she walked into the dining room. Sam looked

29

at us and I realized he was thinking about the fact that Jenny had been bitten.

"We don't know what will happen yet, Jenny." Sam told her.

Sawyer and I walked Jenny to Carter and Marie's room. It took a while to get her to calm down and rest again.

She cried even when she finally fell back to sleep and mumbled about losing her family.

"Ashlyn where are your parents?" Sam asked me as we returned to the dining room.

"They went to some conference in California." I answered.

My heart pounded as I thought about my parents.

I had forgotten they weren't here.

Now all I could think was if I would ever see them again, if they were facing the same things we were here, if they were even alive right now.

"We should try to reach them." Sam said. "Give me their number, I'll try and reach them while I try to reach my nephew."

"Okay." I agreed. My hand shook as I wrote their cell numbers down.

"What about Sawyer's parents?" He asked as he took the paper.

Sawyer started to cry.

"They're camping and river rafting. Supposed to be gone for three weeks." I answered.

Sam left the room to make calls. I sat for a few minutes just taking deep breaths.

Sawyer mumbled something I didn't catch and walked away.

I had to find my cell and try to call my parents.

I was walking past the front door when I heard a soft knock. I looked out of the door scope. I could see the familiar black hair from a neighborhood boy who was three years younger than Sawyer and me. I cracked the door open.

"Axel?" I asked.

"Yeah. Can I come in please? There's things out here." He sounded like he had run all the way here. I let him in and as soon as the door closed he was hugging me and crying.

"Where are your parents?" I asked him, suspecting the worse.

"They're dead. Carter attacked dad, I shot him. His eyes turned red and he went after dad again and killed him. He came after me but mom threw herself at him and told me to run. I didn't know where else to go." Axel sobbed into my shoulder, confirming my suspicions.

"Oh Axel, I'm so sorry." I told him as I hugged him back and let him cry.

"What's happening?" Axel asked as he pulled away and wiped away the evidence of tears.

"We don't know yet, but you're safe here." I told him.

At the sound of footsteps, I turned to find Sam coming our way.

"Were you bit?" Sam asked. He must have heard what had happened to Axel's parents.

"No I wasn't." Axel answered, sounding more like his normal fourteen-year-old self.

"Good. Ashlyn I couldn't get hold of your parents. I did get ahold of my nephew and we are going to round up everyone we can in the neighborhood and head to him." Sam responded.

"Why are we heading to your nephew?" I asked, not really wanting to face the craziness of what was going on beyond the front door.

"Drew and his father built a resort called Paradis Roulette. It's a bio dome. It is solar powered and Drew says that they haven't had any outbreaks like we have. So we'll be safer there till we figure out what's happening." Sam told us.

Chapter Three

I went to check on Jenny before joining the others in the dining room. She was still sleeping in Carter and Marie's room.

Sam, Sawyer, and Axel were already sitting around the dining room table when I walked in.

Sawyer had our chairs pulled next to each other so we could share the large orange throw blanket. Axel chose the seat next to Sam, his hands slowly spinning the cup in front of him. Sam had already explained to them that we were going to try and make it to his nephew's bio dome resort.

"Wait. If we are bringing Jenny with us, aren't we contaminating the dome?" Sawyer asked.

"If she doesn't turn crazed before we can get her there. Drew has his own fully staffed hospital in the dome; we can get her in an isolation room." Sam responded.

"How are we going to get people here to go there?" I asked.

"I'm going to call around and we'll see how many people show up before we leave for the dome." Sam answered, "I'll start with a cop I know, him and his partner may be able to round up some people."

"So what do we do while you make calls?" I asked.

"You can try to get hold of your families." Sam answered as he walked out of the room.

"I'm going to check updates on Facebook." Sawyer decided, "Do you want to come with me to the office?"

"Yeah, maybe we can even find more information online." Axel added as we followed Sawyer down the hall.

Sawyer turned into the office with Axel on her heels. I stayed back near the door and looked at the picture of my parents on my contact list. I tapped my finger on Mom's and listened to the ring.

No answer. Just the voicemail full message.

I tried Dad's next. After three rings it went straight to his voicemail.

"Dad it's me. There's a lot going on here. The neighbor Sam is with me and we are going to Paradis Roulette. Call me please. I love you." I said after the beep.

I tapped my phone off and went to look over Sawyer's shoulder. There were images and videos up that looked similar to what we had seen.

"Turn it off." Axel said.

Sawyer did.

"Let's go back to Sam." Axel called over his shoulder as he headed to find the old cowboy.

Sawyer nodded to my phone and sent me a questioning look as soon as we were alone. I shook my head.

"I'm sorry." She mouthed to me. I wiped the tears that trailed down my face away and followed after Axel.

Sam was pacing around the living room when we walked in.

"Any luck?" I asked.

"He said he was going to find a ride and be here." Sam answered as he made another lap.

He was on the tenth lap when we heard crashing in the back yard.

Peeking through the cracks of the boarded windows we could see a huge bus lined up with the back of the house.

Knocking sounded on the backdoor.

Sawyer and I looked to Sam. He shrugged and went to check it out.

Sawyer grabbed my wrist and dragged me along as she followed.

Sam cracked the door open and looked outside; he started laughing and swung the door the rest of the way open.

"You're lucky this door opens inwards, Tone." Sam greeted the dark-skinned cop. His friendly brown eyes took in the whole room in a quick sweeping glance.

"Yeah, well I was prepared to knock it in if I had to." Tone responded as he came into the kitchen, "There was no way in hell I was bringing her back around to try again."

"Why did you park so close?" Sam asked. He looked out the door and down the length of the bus, "There's not even six inches between the house and that bus."

"Things have gotten nuts out there. We thought it'd be safer to get people loaded in if it was a straight shot." A woman's voice came from just out of sight.

Once Sam stepped out of the way a woman with black hair came out to stand next to Tone, she was a good foot shorter than him.

"Good to see you Sydney." Sam said to her as he hugged her.

"I know on the phone you said you wanted to leave in the morning but as Syd said, its nuts and we're going now while we can." Tone announced.

"Okay, Sawyer please go get Jenny and Axel." Sam directed, "Ashlyn go start grabbing supplies."

Sam kept everyone busy. He had us gathering what we could. Clothes, food, blankets, pillows, batteries, and anything else we could fit. When we'd finally emptied the house of useful supplies he had us load onto the bus.

There was a girl asleep on the couch when we boarded. Her back was to the living room area of the bus so all we could see was that she had long emerald green hair.

The bus itself was huge. There was no way this thing was your typical stock model from a lot.

There was a living room with a hallway leading down one way and a kitchen on the other side. Tone was heading to the kitchen through an open door that looked to be the front of the bus.

"Okay everybody, let's get you all settled in." Sydney told us as we started rolling. She led

Jenny down the hallway to what must have been a bedroom.

Axel curled up in a recliner near the couch. Sawyer and I sat down in chairs around a dining room table. I was watching the green-haired girl wondering who she was.

"A tour bus, really?" Sam asked Tone as he went through the door to the front of the bus.

"Yeah, I can drive the beast and the girl back there was trapped in it after an outbreak at her band's concert." Tone answered, "She said she never saw what happened to her band mates and she can't drive this."

Sam closed the door shutting him and Tone off from the rest of us. Sydney returned from the back of the bus and sat down in the chair across from me.

"We haven't been introduced, I'm Sydney Tyme, my partner is Antonio Varqez, he goes by Tone. The girl on the couch is Daisy Duke." Sydney said.

"Wait, Daisy Duke as in Daisy Chain's Daisy Duke?" Sawyer asked, lifting her head from the table.

"Yeah, like Tone said she was trapped in here. He thought it would be easier to travel in." Sydney answered. "I'll introduce you when she wakes up."

"Oh I'm Sawyer Raide by the way." Sawyer responded.

"I'm Ashlyn Glass." I added "And the boy sleeping on the recliner is Axel Bishop."

Sydney showed Sawyer and me to one of the bedrooms on the bus; it was the first room on the left. Jenny was in the room directly at the end of the hallway.

"I know the rooms aren't big but at least there's a bed to sleep on." Sydney said as we crawled onto the full size built in that touched both walls.

"Thank you. Is one of the rooms yours?" I asked.

"Yeah, I took the room right across the hall from you and Daisy's room is the other door on this side." Sydney answered "You two should try and get some sleep. Do you want the door open or closed?"

"Open." Sawyer decided for us.

I didn't think I would be able to sleep, but the last noise I heard was a door closing.

Dreams were scattered. Images of Marie and Carter dressed up walking out the door. Blood. Mom with her camera. Screams. Dad holding tissue ready for when Mom grabbed it. A man being ran over by a red car.

My parents with their eyes glowing red.

I woke to my pillow wet with my tears and the image of my parents haunting me.

Sawyer was asleep so I slid out of the bed careful not to wake her and joined the few people who were awake. In the living room Axel was up and playing Trivial Pursuit with Daisy.

"Morning." I said as I sat next to Axel on the floor.

"Hey." Axel responded first.

"Back at ya." Daisy responded, "You must be Ashlyn."

"That would be me." I told her, "How'd you guess?"

"Axel said you had brown hair. Want to play?" Daisy asked me even though it looked like they had already been playing for a while. "We can restart or you could just jump in."

I wasn't comfortable sitting on the floor playing a game while the world outside was going to hell in a hand basket.

Sam came and sat on the couch, silent for a few moments.

"We are going to make a stop for supplies." Sam told us.

"A stop where?" Daisy asked.

"A gas station to fuel up then a department store for anything the gas station doesn't have."

Sam responded, "We'll stop at whatever one we see first to load up on any necessities we need."

"How is a gas station going to have anything we need?" Daisy asked again. It seemed like the idea of stopping freaked her out. Sam seemed to pick up on the same thing.

"It'll be a quick stop and you won't have to get off the bus if you don't want to." Sam told her as he knelt in front of her with his hand on her shoulder.

"Promise it'll be quick?" Daisy asked.

"I promise." Sam agreed.

"Then I'm coming in too." Daisy said, she held her head up and rolled her shoulders back.

Chapter Four

Tone pulled the bus up to the pumps. Sydney and Sam were checking their guns. Sawyer and Axel didn't want to go into the station. Jenny came and sat on the couch. She looked disoriented and her hair was all over her face.

"Sam, you know how to turn the pumps on?" Tone called from the driver's seat.

"Yeah, you pump while we grab what supplies we can." Sam called back.

"Okay, could you check out the RV parked on the other pump too?" Tone asked.

"Yeah we got it." Sydney responded as she loaded her gun into its holster on her hip.

Daisy pulled her long green hair into a ponytail and followed Sam to the store. I went with Sydney to check out the RV.

The sky was gathering clouds and the breeze smelt of rain. I remembered it was called *petrichor* from some Greek mythology teachers thought we needed to know.

I stood next to Sydney looking at the campsite picture on the RV and couldn't figure out how knowing Greek mythology helped me now.

"Stay behind me when we get inside." Sydney told me as we got closer to the huge unnecessary vehicle people pretended to camp in.

"Okay. What are we going to do if we find people?" I asked as she took the lead so I was looking at her black hair in its ponytail.

"I don't know." Sydney answered as she reached up to try the door.

Surprisingly it was unlocked and opened easily.

The place was empty. There were no dishes scattered around or clothes. Nothing to show that someone had been here.

"This is pointless." I said as I picked at the hem of my shirt.

"Shhh." Sydney hushed me, "Did you hear that?"

"Hear what?" I asked.

She was already moving to the closed door in the back. She signaled me to stay where I was, but I followed her anyway.

Tilting my head towards the door I could hear the faint crying on the other side.

"You don't have to be afraid. My name is Sydney and I am a cop. Are you hurt?" Sydney called softly through the door.

There was no response for a while.

"Are the other people gone?" Finally came through the door.

"What other people?" Sydney called back.

"The ones who attacked us. They were everywhere and they were biting and eating people." The response came.

"There's no one here except for the group I am traveling with. You can come out we won't hurt you." Sydney called, her hand resting on the door.

The door opened slowly revealing a girl with short brown hair. She looked to be about fourteen and she was holding the hand of a little boy. Both their eyes were green and wide, the little boy was still crying.

"Hi sweetie what's your name?" Sydney asked the girl as she crouched down in front of the boy.

"I'm Angela and he's Thomas. Do you know where our parents are?" Angela asked.

"We didn't see anyone else. When did you last see them?" Sydney asked.

"When we were attacked. They made us stay and hide here, they said they'd be back, but they had to make sure we would be safe first." Angela responded, her tears slipping down her cheeks.

Sydney looked over her shoulder at me and I could tell we were both thinking the same thing. The chances of their parents still being alive were slim to none.

"Let's get you two onto our bus and Ashlyn and I will take a look around to see if your parents found a safe place to hide." Sydney suggested, taking Angela's hand. Angela nodded and followed us out of the RV. Tone was pumping the gas into the bus as we walked up. Sydney left Angela and Thomas with me as she went to fill Tone in on what we had learned.

Angela was looking around when she started screaming. At first I didn't see anything, but then I saw where she was looking.

Daisy and Sam were running towards us and right behind them were people with red eyes.

I pushed Angela and Thomas towards the bus and they ran but I didn't think Sam and Daisy were going to make it back to the bus. I could hear Sawyer screaming on the bus but couldn't hear what she was saying.

I was looking behind me when hands grabbed me and shoved towards the bus and someone was running past me towards Sam and Daisy. I focused on Jenny drawing the attention of the Red Eyes as she threw herself into the group of them.

They converged on her. She never screamed and within seconds she was gone under the mass of the group of Red Eyes. Sam grabbed my arm and dragged me after him back onto the bus that Tone already had running. As soon as we boarded he started driving.

"What about Jenny?" Sawyer cried, staring out the window where the pile of Red Eyes was still squirming.

"She's gone." Sam told her looking in the same direction.

"So we're not even going to try?" Sawyer yelled at Sam.

"Now listen, she sacrificed herself to give us all a chance to get out of there. You remember that." Sam told her, "You give thanks. But she is past us being able to help her. Look at that pile— I don't think there's even going to be enough of her left to rise when the Red Eyes are done."

Sam grabbed her shoulders and forced her to look at him. Sawyer melted into him crying and he held her rocking her back and forth.

"It'll be okay Sawyer. We'll all be okay." Sam was whispering to her as she cried.

We moved Angela and Thomas into the room Jenny had stayed in.

Neither one of them said much, the only thing we could do was let them process. I wanted to hope their parents had survived, but I knew they had more than likely went the same way Jenny had.

I tried to take comfort in what Sam had said and believe Jenny wouldn't come back. But I knew in my dreams she would be there with red eyes.

Axel stayed by Sawyer's side since she had curled up on the couch. He was holding her hand as she stared off into nothing. Sam said she'd be okay in time. She was just processing what had happened.

At this rate I wondered if we would even make it to Paradis Roulette. Sam seemed determined. He had disappeared up to the front of the bus with Tone and they had the door shut. So whatever they were discussing we weren't aware of. I figured they were planning our route and dealing with the loss of Jenny.

"Hey." Daisy said as she sat down next to me on the bed.

"Hey." I responded.

"I'm sorry about your friend." Daisy told me.

"She wasn't really my friend. Sawyer dated her son and she ended up with us after her husband went crazed at my sister's celebration of life. In the chaos she ended up with us. I feel horrible that I didn't try to get to know her." I answered, spilling out things I hadn't even realized I was feeling.

"She seemed pretty brave, I mean she really didn't know me but if it weren't for her I wouldn't be here. She had to have known what would happen to her by running out like that." Daisy said as she looked at her hands.

"So what happened in the store?" I asked her. Neither she nor Sam had said anything about what had happened before the group of Red Eyes attacked.

"Sam turned the pump on and started gathering supplies. I think Jenny is my fault." She confessed.

"How would that be your fault?" I asked her.

"I wasn't getting supplies. I was looking for those little shoe figurines they sell everywhere to add to my collection." She was crying, "I knocked over a shelf and the noise must have attracted the Red Eyes from the back room. Sam barely got me out of there. I risked our lives and caused Jenny to lose hers for a glass shoe that I somehow managed to hold on to through all that."

"Daisy, you can't blame yourself. You didn't know there were Red Eyes in the store and Jenny made a choice for whatever reasons she had." I told her as I put my hand on hers.

"I just feel like if I was doing what Sam had told me to do we would have made it out of there without being attacked." She said.

"Maybe. Or maybe not. It could have ended up that way no matter what. All we can really do now is stick together and make it to Paradis Roulette. Hopefully Sam is right and we'll be safe there." I said to try and comfort her, "Tell me about the shoes."

"I've collected them ever since my dad walked out on us when I was nine. My older brother, Luke, started bringing them home for me. He still brings me new ones whenever we get to see each other." Daisy told me.

"That's cool that he was there for you and that you have something special with him." I responded.

"Yeah, but I also don't know if he's safe, or if he's dead, or worse, if he's one of those freaks now." She said, "I thought about going to try and find him but I don't even know where to start."

"We can talk to Sam once we get to Paradis Roulette, he may have an idea to help get other survivors to safety. At least if it really is safe there." I told her.

"Do you really think Sam will help find my brother?" She asked, sounding hopeful.

"Yes, I think he will once we get to safety." I responded and Daisy hugged me.

It was surreal having someone from one of my favorite bands sitting on a bed with me. I never thought of her as a real person before, she was this huge deal up on stage or touring, adored by fans.

Although now we were on the same level. We both survived and were trying to figure out how we keep doing so. As well as doing our part in keeping the whole group alive.

"Hey girls, I wanted to let you know we're going to make another stop soon for more supplies as well as weapons." Sam said from the doorway, "We want to be prepared so we aren't caught off guard like that again."

Chapter Five

Neither Daisy nor I wanted to be alone as we laid on her bed looking at the ceiling. She had a poster of the General Lee taped there. We were quiet. Thinking about what Sam had said and wondering if we'd ever be safe.

"Where do you think they're planning to stop?" Daisy asked.

"Someplace that's abandoned, I hope." I answered.

"Agreed. Do you mind staying in here with me tonight since it seems like Sawyer's staying on the couch?" She asked as she fiddled with a strand of her green hair that had come out of the ponytail.

"Yeah, I don't really want to be alone." I answered.

Daisy fell asleep before I did. I listened to her even breathing for a while hoping it would lull me into sleep.

It was no use I could feel my heart pounding.

My mind was racing with scenarios we may or may not face at the next stop.

Morning came bright and glorious, I felt like I had just fallen asleep when knocking sounded on the door.

"What?" Daisy called from under her pillow.

"Rise and shine girls." Sam called back and opened the door.

The smell of eggs cooking wafted through the open door as we pulled ourselves away from the warm blankets. I stumbled out to the kitchen to find Tone standing at the stove. The handle of the pan in one hand and a spatula in the other. The closed cabinets around him had hook locks on them, I hadn't noticed that before.

"What are you looking at?" Daisy asked.

"Just noticed the cabinet doors." I answered.

"What about them?" She asked.

"The locks." I said.

"Well yeah, how else would the food and everything stay in them while the bus is moving?" She responded.

"Ah." I said as I took the plate Tone handed to me.

Sawyer was still lying on the couch. Although Axel was now sitting on the chair, with a plate on his lap. Sydney smiled at both Daisy and me as we sat down at the dining room table with her.

Angela came out and grabbed a plate but she returned to her and Thomas's room without saying a word to anyone. She was skittish around us. It was the first time we'd really seen her since she got on the bus. We hadn't seen her brother at all.

"They'll come around." Sydney said as Angela closed the door.

"Wonder how long they were out there and how much of the attack they saw." Daisy responded looking at the door. "They're staying in Johnnie's room."

"Johnnie was the drummer, wasn't he?" I asked her.

"Yeah. He threw me into the bus and made me promise not to go back out. I can still hear him screaming, I couldn't get the door open he jammed it somehow." Daisy replied. "I never

53

even saw that there was danger near the bus; I thought we had left it at the stage."

"He saved you." I said.

"He did. Tone and Sydney found me in here when they opened the door." Daisy answered, "I hope she didn't see or hear as much as I did."

"Do you know what happened to the rest of the band?" Axel asked.

"I saw Robert get pulled down off the stage, Johnnie was with me. Andrew, I lost in the chaos. He didn't come back to the bus and I don't know if he's dead or alive." Daisy told him.

"I saw my parents get attacked." Axel told her.

She nodded and hugged him to her.

"Do you think there are other groups like ours?" Daisy asked.

"Probably and maybe we'll even find some more people on our way and they'll join us." Tone answered.

"I hope so." Sam said, clapping Tone on the shoulder.

It was easy to not look out the windows and ignore that we were on a trip trying to make it to safety. We all had loved ones lost we tried not to think about. Some we knew were gone, others we weren't sure about. We knew we had to keep our minds on surviving and not forget what the bus protected us from.

"There's a Super Wal-Mart a few miles up the road from where we are right now." Tone started, "We plan to stop, get supplies and check for survivors."

"We understand if you want to stay on the bus, but the more eyes we have inside the safer we will all be." Sam continued.

"Everyone would stay in a group no separating unless absolutely necessary. We still need to make sure we have food and water for our trip." Tone added on, "There may be others that have no place to go."

Both Daisy and I volunteered to go. Axel said he'd stay with Sawyer on the bus and keep an eye on her. Having the scavenging group decided, Tone got back behind the wheel and we started off towards the store.

The trip was quicker than I would have liked. I was afraid we would be walking into the same situation as the gas station. I guess this time we were at least prepared for running into Red Eyes.

Sam gave us some wicked looking hunting knives. The weight of the knife was comforting as we pulled into the parking lot that looked like a mass accident.

There were cars everywhere and you could see dead people in some of them.

The worst one was a child hanging out of a window, half of him gone.

There was a lot of blood everywhere like some Hollywood movie, only no one was going to be calling cut. Sam took in everything as he looked around us.

Tone pulled the bus up to the front of the store making sure he had a clear path to get us back out of the parking lot. Nothing was moving, not even a breeze.

"Okay, we are going to do this quickly. Head to camping first. Grab what we can and any bags we can." Sam directed, "Then go through the store hitting food last so we have an easy time getting back to the bus."

"Remember we are grabbing anything we need, so medicines, bandages, clothes, food and such. Stay together. Ready?" Tone asked us as we stood by the door, waiting.

"Here we go." Sydney said as she stepped off the bus and we followed her.

Sydney took the lead, Sam was in the middle with Daisy and I, while Tone took up the rear. The doors to the store were crushed and once we were inside we found a car someone had driven through the glass.

Other than the car, the store wasn't as torn up as I was expecting it to be. The lights were out and it was hard to see clearly past the light from the wrecked door. Maybe I just had the images from too many horror movies in my head. I was expecting shelves to be mostly looted and knocked over.

Everything still seemed to be in fairly good order as we made our way to camping supplies. We grabbed a few carts on the way and as we continued deeper into the store, our eyes adjusted to the dark.

We started seeing spots that were dark, like oil spills, but we all knew they probably weren't oil. Halfway through the store Sam tripped over what was left of someone's arm.

Once we got to the camping aisle we saw that there were two bodies lying at the other end. It was too dark to tell if they were male or female. Tone went to check the bodies; he came back shaking his head.

"Are they going to come back?" I asked, not wanting to face Red Eyes in the close quarters of the aisle.

"No, there's not enough left for them to rise." Tone answered, taking a tarp and throwing it over them.

"Let's get lanterns, knives, and tents if there are any left." Sam said. He looked like he was on high alert.

There was only one tent left on the shelf and it was one of those huge four room ones. The lanterns on the other hand, looked like no one else had even touched them so we took all of them. Sam had us grab tarps and sleeping bags while he loaded up cases of bottled water that were right on the end of the aisle.

We had one cart completely loaded when Sam took us over to electronics to grab any and all batteries we could.

We did the same at home improvement grabbing ropes, chains, and tie downs. Trying to ignore bodies or limbs.

We followed Sam over to the pharmacy.

He hopped over the counter and started grabbing things from there. The rest of us just started throwing everything we could off the shelves into the cart. Not even looking at what we grabbed.

We did the same with clothing until we had all three of the carts piled way past capacity. We headed back to the doors to pass off the carts to Sawyer and Axel, then grabbed new ones to head over to the food aisles.

We were scooping canned food off the shelves into carts when we heard something hiss at us.

Sydney turned on a small flashlight she had on her belt and shone it in the direction the noise had come from. Huddled as far from the light as the back wall of the store would allow were three people.

As soon as Sydney moved the light away, a male lunged at us only to slip on a wet spot on the floor. A drop fell from the ceiling on to him and he screamed and ran off closely followed by the two other people. Sydney shined the light up where there was water dripping down, maybe from a busted pipe. There was a ladder and one of those wet floor signs near the puddle.

"I'm guessing crazed." Sam decided as he turned around to head back to the front of the store.

"Why are they afraid of light and water?" Daisy asked.

"I'm not sure but we'll keep that in mind." Sam answered, motioning us to follow him. He was leading back to the bus when we heard something above us in the ceiling. Tone had a finger to his mouth telling us to stay quiet. Sydney went to investigate.

She came back shaking her head at us.

"Let's hurry and get the hell out of here." Sydney said.

"What did you find?" Tone asked her.

"Red Eyes upstairs in the employee area, must have chased someone up there and had no reason to come back down." Sydney told him.

"In that case, I think we've got plenty, let's go before we give them a reason to come down here." Tone said.

We were quiet as we headed back to the doors. I saw a display that had those shoe figurines Daisy had been talking about. Without thinking about it I swiped all the ones I could off it and into a bag I found on the ground. I hurried to catch up with the group.

Sydney came back and grabbed the cart from me. As I walked with her I tripped and stumbled into the car parked by the door. The car had one of those stupid overly sensitive alarms that started to scream at us.

Tone looked up from loading up supplies and grabbed his gun. Sydney and I rushed back to the bus with the cart.

At first all we could hear was the damn alarm, and then there was crashing as the Red Eyes were drawn to the noise. The alarm seemed to even draw the attention of Red Eyes that were walking by.

We left the last of the supplies and rushed to load back into the bus as the first of the Red Eyes started rushing towards us. Tone jumped into the driver seat. Sam slammed the door shut.

"Go, go, go!" he screamed to Tone.

The engine revved up and we pulled away from the store. You could hear the Red Eyes running into the side of the bus trying to catch us. The bus bounced around over bumps that I had a sick feeling were bodies of some of the Red Eyes. I was shaking as Tone got the bus back on to the road and away from chaos once again.

"Everyone okay?" Sam asked as he sat next to me and took my hand into his.

"Yeah. No one's hurt." Sydney answered him.

"I thought they were going to get us when that alarm started going off." Daisy said as she sat down on my other side, "What's in the bag?"

"I grabbed something you might like." I said, handing her the bag.

"What?" Daisy asked. She looked inside.

"Oh my god!" Daisy said as her eyes lit up and she smiled.

"Before you say anything Sam I didn't wander off to find those, they were right where we were walking." I told him before he could lecture me.

"You know what, we should be enjoying the small things and we should be trying to make each other as happy as we can. We have no idea what lays ahead of us now." Sam told me, "Plus you're right you didn't wander away and draw attention to us."

Sawyer came out from the room we shared. She took one look at me and threw herself into my arms.

"Hey, are you okay?" I asked her when she didn't let go.

"Yeah, it just hit me how much we've lost. I heard that alarm going off and I thought I was going to lose you too." Sawyer told me as she sat back. I was glad to see her up and moving around, out of shock.

"I'm sorry I scared you." I told her.

"How long will it take us to get to your nephew?" Sawyer asked.

"Paradis Roulette is close to 150 miles from here. It depends on what's between here and there." Sam responded and patted her on the head. "The important thing we have to remember is to stick together and help each other."

When we had all calmed down from the near miss in the Super Wal-Mart, Sydney made us all peanut butter and raspberry jelly sandwiches for lunch. She even took one to the front of the bus for Tone to munch on while he drove. Then she came and sat down to eat her own. Sam cleared his throat getting all our attentions.

"What did we see inside the store?" Sam asked.

"Blood and bodies." Daisy answered, taking another bite.

"Notice anything about that?" Sam asked.

"No, what should we have?" I asked, wondering what he had seen that we hadn't.

"The bodies weren't just chewed up like the Red Eyes do; it looked like tools were used on them." Tone called from the front.

"Exactly. Which leads me to believe that the crazed aren't as far gone as the Red Eyes are. It's like they were almost trying to cut pieces like you would a cow." Sam responded.

"Bringing up the crazed, what the hell was up with the water and light fear?" Daisy asked as she finished eating and leaned forward intently.

"I'm still not sure about that. Maybe they've been in the dark for a while and the light hurt their eyes. The water may have just caught them off guard." Sam answered, "I can't think of anything that would make something afraid of water. Although, maybe Drew will know when we get to Paradis Roulette."

"I hope we get there soon. Seems like the longer it takes the crazier things get." I said, not to anyone in particular more thinking aloud.

"It depends what we run into on the way, who knows what we're facing and what will slow this trip down." Sydney responded wrapping her arm around my shoulders.

"Was it really that horrible in the store?" Sawyer asked, speaking for the first time since we had all sat down.

"Yeah it was like some horror movie only covering your eyes didn't make it go away." Daisy answered.

"It also means that wherever we stop we have to be careful and stick together, some places could be worse." Sam said.

"Are we going to have to stop again?" Axel asked. He was fiddling with a piece of crust he hadn't eaten yet.

"We might, depends if we see someone who needs help, or we need gas, or we realize we need something we don't have." Sam told him, patting his knee to comfort him.

Everyone went quiet for a while, lost in their own thoughts.

I was watching the landscape going by out the window. The side of the road was lined with cars that looked abandoned. I didn't want to look too closely at them. I'd rather believe their owners walked away from them, then see something inside them.

Sam didn't seem too interested in stopping to check them out either. There was no point to go and look when we saw no movement. All we might find were trapped Red Eyes in them and we would be putting ourselves in danger.

I found myself heading back to my room, tired of watching cars go by outside I wanted to lay down and maybe sleep. Sawyer and Daisy both followed me and all of us ended up on the bed kind of laying on each other.

Axel came in a short while later and found a spot for himself with his head on Daisy's stomach. None of us said anything; we took comfort from each other doing something teens did all the time.

Chapter Six

I woke still in the pile and the bus wasn't moving. I looked for a clock automatically, but the only one in the room was a digital alarm clock. The display was dead, which was just a reminder that not even time mattered anymore.

I could hear the adults talking softly in the living room. As I sat up I noticed that Angela and Thomas had come in and joined us. They were sitting on the foot of the bed together, but it was more than they had done so far. They both sat there watching us with matching green eyes. Daisy rolled and saw them too.

"Well, hi there." Daisy greeted them like you would a frightened animal.

"Hi." Thomas squeaked, talking for the first time since we had found them.

"How are you two holding up?" Sawyer asked, looking directly at Angela.

Angela shrugged.

She looked calm, unless you looked at her twisting, clutching hands, then you could see what she was feeling. She was putting on a brave face for her brother, but she looked like she wanted to cry.

"I lost my sister and I have no idea if my parents are safe or not." I told her, "You really have to try and focus on here and now and we'll deal with whatever else there is together."

"Together?" Angela asked, looking at me like I was a lifeline.

"Yeah, you're part of our group now." I answered.

"Not group." Axel said, "Our family."

"You know what? I like that." Sawyer agreed. Soon all of us were teasing each other as we convinced Angela and Thomas to join the pile we had going on the bed.

Our talking brought Sydney to check on us. She stood with her hip against the door frame watching us. She didn't say anything but she was smiling, and seemed a bit surprised that Angela and Thomas had joined us.

"What are you all doing?" She asked after a while.

"Just hanging out." Daisy responded as she fought to get into a sitting position.

"How did you all manage to fit on that bed?" Sydney seemed genuinely curious.

"Very carefully." I answered.

"Well, can you manage to untangle yourselves and come eat some dinner?" Sydney asked.

Sydney watched as one by one we all managed to wiggle our way free of the pile we had made. She seemed pleased that Angela and Thomas didn't disappear back into their room. They ventured with us to the living room to see what was for dinner. Tone was cooking at the stove when we all sat down in various spots.

"Heard you laughing back there, was about to come join you when Sydney put my ass to work." He said and smiled at us, winking when Sydney looked away.

"Well somebody has to keep you in line Tone." Sam called from the front of the bus.

"You see how they gang up on me?" Tone asked us, trying his best to look hurt.

"They see plenty." Sydney said.

It was easy to see why Axel called us family.

Tone and Sydney worked around each other in the kitchen. The smell of the chicken on the stove made my mouth water as we waited.

Thomas had taken a liking to Sam and was sitting on his lap while Axel showed Angela the board game collection. We had a break from the chaos going on outside.

A gun fired.

I went to the windows with Sam and Tone. Outside, we saw a group of men with two female Red Eyes. They had the Red Eyes muzzled. Their hands were zip tied behind their backs. There was also some of handmade harness around their upper bodies that the men had leashes attached to.

Sam signaled for us all to be quiet. He opened a window so we could hear what was going on without alerting the men to our presence.

"I told you this would work." One of the men said, he had tribal looking tattoos going up his arms.

"Yeah, you were right." a man with shaved head said and laughed.

"I told you they wouldn't look beat up, hell they almost look alive." The tattooed men said as he reached out and slapped one of the Red Eyes on her butt. She tried to turn and snap at him, but the whole get up they had to prevent that, worked. "Say no to me now bitch."

Tattooed guy's friends were all laughing. I counted four of them. One of the guys was wearing what looked to be a police officer's shirt while the other had a plain black T-shirt on. They were all taking turns caressing the bound Red Eyes.

It seemed that the men had known the two girls before they got turned. These men had found them, and were planning to have sex with them even though they were dead. The thought was appalling, who would be willing to do anything with a Red Eye besides run like hell?

No wonder the women had turned them down while they were alive, these guys were creeps. I noticed there was a fifth man that was staying further away from the group. He didn't appear to be laughing at their jokes.

"Sam, you hearing this?" Tone whispered.

"Yeah." Sam whispered back.

"We can't let them rape those girls." Tone responded.

"They are dead." Sam said, looking at Tone like he was gauging him.

"You know that doesn't matter. They don't deserve to be treated or disrespected that way. The world order may not be where it was, but there is still a very solid line between right and wrong." Tone said meeting Sam's eyes.

"I agree." Sam responded.

"So let's go rescue some Red Eyes." Sydney agreed as the conversation continued outside.

"Hey Aaron let's see if we can get one of these cars started so we can get home quicker and have some fun." Tattooed guy called to the guy with his hood covering his face, he was also staying away from the group.

"Yeah, how about that cop car over there?" Aaron responded scratching his head and looking around. The voice sounded familiar, but I couldn't place where I knew it from.

Tattooed guy was laughing as he dragged the Red Eyes behind him towards the abandoned cop car. He only stopped to pull out a knife that he handed to the guy in the police shirt. He used it to cut open the shirt of the blonde Red Eye. Revealing a hot pink bra and some small tattoos right above her hip bones. Aaron kept moving to the cop car, not looking back at what his companions were doing.

"When we go out there we need all of you to stay on the bus and stay quiet." Tone told us.

"We will." I told him.

"These guys may be pervs but they are still human, let's try not to kill them if we can." Sydney said as she checked the clip in her gun.

"What are you going to do with the Red Eyes?" Axel asked.

"Kill them humanely." Sam answered as he returned his gun to the holster on his hip.

The three of them climbed out the door silently. They started the trek of slipping behind abandoned cars as they snuck up on the group. Aaron had the cop car door open and was messing with the dash. His companions continued to cut select pieces of clothing off the Red Eyes.

Tone had taken the lead and was inching closer to tattooed guy; he was a couple of cars away now. Tattooed guy didn't even know Tone was there until he cut the leash he was holding to keep the two Red Eyes with him. Sydney stepped up behind the Red Eyes and despite tattooed guy screaming at her, she shot both of them in the head.

At the sounds of shots, the guy in the police shirt went running followed by the guy with the shaved head. Tattooed guy grabbed a gun from a holster on his hip and aimed it at Sydney as the Red Eyes dropped. He fired. Tone jumped, knocking Sydney out of the way, but we saw the blood spray from where he got hit. Sydney returned fire hitting tattooed guy in the forehead. He went down as Sam approached, his gun trained on the guy in the black shirt. Aaron stood up slowly from the car with his hands in the air.

"Don't shoot." Aaron called.

"Don't move." Sam responded, "Syd, he okay?"

"From what I can see he is. Bullet went clear through his shoulder." Sydney answered as she helped Tone up and started walking him back to the bus.

The guy in the black shirt drew his gun and aimed it at Sam, but just as quickly Aaron had a gun out and shot him. Sam looked at Aaron for a minute before he nodded.

"Grab a tarp when you come back out." Sam called after her.

Sydney brought Tone back onto the bus. She directed Sawyer on how to clean the wound, while she grabbed a tarp and headed back to Sam.

"Cover the girls." Sam told her and she did.

"Could you cover my brother too?" Aaron asked, "He's the one with the tattoos." Sam nodded to Sydney and she covered tattooed guy with an end of the tarp. She kept him as far away from the Red Eyes as the tarp allowed.

"What were you all doing?" Sam asked Aaron, still holding the gun pointed at him.

"Man, I don't know what Wayne was thinking, but once he got something in his head it was better just to go along with it. He was a mean son of a bitch if you tried to oppose him on anything." Aaron said, "I didn't want to do it so he found his drinking buddies and still had me tag along."

Not being able to place the voice was bugging me.

"What did he have you do?" Sam asked.

"See, we met these two girls at the bar a few nights back before the world went balls deep crazy. Wayne, now he really liked that blonde, think her name was Cat or something, but the redhead kept getting in his way." Aaron said as he lowered his arms to his sides.

"How does that get us here?" Sam asked.

"I'm getting there. He bought her drinks and was trying to get Cat to go home with him but she said no. He was pissed and still reeling about it when we found the girls after being bit last night." Aaron explained. "Wayne told them he'd help them and they would be okay they just had to come home with us where he had the supplies. He got them to this house and down to the basement."

Aaron took a breath and looked between Sam and Sydney.

"Wayne got them to let him zip tie their hands. He told them it was for his safety, since cleaning the bites was going to hurt. Soon as their hands were tied he knocked them out." He continued.

"What happened then?" Sydney asked.

"He started strangling the redhead. I told him to stop but he told me it didn't matter they'd been bit they were dead anyway." Aaron answered. "He strangled Cat too, than made those muzzles and those harnesses. I know what he wanted to do was wrong but he's my big brother and he's never listened to me."

"That's quite a tale there Aaron. You just confessed to watching your brother kill two women." Sam responded to Aaron's story.

"As I said I didn't want nothing to do with it. I tried to calm Wayne down but he's a mean guy and he holds a grudge like a starved dog holds a bone." Aaron explained, "Please don't kill me. I swear I didn't touch the girls nor was I going to. I was planning to take off as soon as he was distracted."

"Well now, what should we do with you Aaron?" Sam asked, lowering his gun finally.

"Take me with you? I can help with your friend Wayne shot, I've cleaned wounds like that before." Aaron said after he thought about it for a moment.

"How do we know you're not going to try and get revenge on us for killing your brother?

We've got kids with us trusting us to keep them safe." Sam asked him.

"As I said. The world's gone crazy and Wayne wasn't someone I would have saved if I could, even with him being my brother." Aaron answered.

"Sydney, cuff him." Sam decided, "It wouldn't be right to leave him alone out here."

"Thank you." Aaron said as he turned around and placed his hands behind his back. Sydney handcuffed him and they led him onto the bus.

Once they got Aaron on the bus they took off the handcuffs so he could take a look at Tone. He pushed his hood down and looked up. My eyes met his blue-green ones, eyes I'd seen a hundred times before.

"Ashlyn?" He asked after a minute.

"Yeah." I answered and went to hug him, "Where's Emily?"

"She's dead." Aaron said and his eyes looked like they were watering up.

Emily was his younger sister and one of my friends. Aaron adored Emily. I remembered how many times he would give us rides or money or anything else she asked him for.

"How?" I asked as tears started to escape from my eyes.

"I don't know. Wayne said she refused to go with him. He wanted to meet with me and she attacked him when he tried to grab her, he said it was an accident." Aaron answered.

"Your brother killed your sister?" Sawyer asked as she joined us, she had been friends with Emily too.

"Yeah he did." Aaron said and turned to look at Tone.

"How does it look?" Tone asked.

"Sorry my brother shot you." He apologized. "Woman was right. Bullet went straight through, I don't think we'll have to do much to help it heal just bandage it and keep it clean. He'll be good as new soon."

"Well then, you hungry?" Tone asked Aaron after he finished getting Tone bandaged up.

"Yeah, been walking all night." Aaron answered and sat down at the table. He looked at Sawyer and me.

"I'm guessing you all know my name how bout you tell me yours." Aaron said and smiled at me.

"Well we got Daisy with the green hair. Axel is right next to her." I told him nodding in their direction. "Angela is holding her brother Thomas. Tone you patched up, Sydney is the woman standing by the doorway, and Sam."

Aaron nodded and ate the food Sydney put down in front of him. He was like an animal deciding what he thought of us and how he should react. He seemed to calm down a bit when Sam took the wheel and started driving the bus.

Tone was asleep in the passenger seat next to him. I think he thought we were going to leave him out there to fend for himself. I don't think Sam could have done that. Even if Aaron had been involved with what his brother was doing and not just a bystander.

"How do you know the girls?" Sydney asked him.

"They were friends with my sister Emily. I used to give them rides everywhere they wanted." Aaron answered.

"You got a last name?" Sydney asked him after he had cleared his plate.

"Yeah, Pierce." Aaron answered.

"That sounds familiar. You ever spend time in the drunk tank?" Sydney asked him.

"No, I didn't but Wayne was a regular there." Aaron answered, a shadow of pain running across his eyes.

"I'm sorry about your brother, we didn't plan to hurt any of you, but he shot my partner, I reacted." Sydney told him.

"I think the shock is wearing off a bit. You have to understand, it's not like we were buds, it was mostly he said jump, I asked how high to avoid a beating." Aaron admitted.

Aaron sat at the dining room table as the bus rumbled down the road. He seemed to be taking in his surroundings and adapting to the new turns that had been taken.

"Ashlyn?" He asked.

"Yeah?" I responded.

"I see Battleship over there. Want to play?" he asked me and I grabbed the game. We set up on the table and started to play.

Chapter Seven

Aaron slept on the couch and was up before any of us, making breakfast. The smell woke me and I followed my nose out to the kitchen and sat at the dining room table watching Aaron. He had shrimp cooking in a skillet as he chopped up mini sweet peppers. He had supplies sitting on the counter next to him. He had a bottle of Ranch, a bottle of Tabasco sauce, bacon, eggs, and shredded mozzarella cheese.

"Good morning." He greeted me as I watched him.

"Morning, what are you making?" I asked him, watching as he cracked eggs open and poured them into another skillet.

"I'm making Cajun eggs and bacon. It's a thank you for letting me stay with you guys." Aaron answered as he started to mix in the mozzarella, and the mini peppers into the skillet with the eggs.

After stirring he added in the shrimp, some ranch, and some tabasco sauce then he covered the skillet. He threw the bacon on to the skillet he'd used for the shrimp.

"It smells great." I told him as Sawyer, Daisy, and Sydney joined us in the kitchen.

"I'll say it does." Sydney agreed.

"It's nothing. I just want to be useful." Aaron answered.

"What if you don't like spicy stuff?" Axel asked from behind Sydney. Angela and Thomas were standing with him as he eyeballed the tabasco sauce.

"Don't you worry; I didn't add enough in to make it spicy. Put in just enough to give it the flavor." Aaron answered as he started dishing out plates to everyone before getting his own plate.

He even brought Sam and Tone plates to the front of the bus. No one spoke much as they ate which says a lot about what everyone thought of Aaron's cooking. He was right that the eggs were not spicy at all but had all the flavor of being so.

Sydney cleaned up the kitchen when everyone was done eating. Aaron sat down on the living room floor to play Life with Axel and Angela while Thomas watched. Sam had

81

decided to take the wheel since he wanted to get a move on. We were driving down the road again. The ride was going smooth for about half an hour before Sam stopped.

"Damn it." Was all he said.

"What's going on?" Sydney asked as she made her way to the front of the bus.

We all looked outside wondering what was going on now. In front of us on the road were a bunch of abandoned cars. A couple buses, an RV, a moving truck, and a semi-truck completely blocking the road.

"Shit. What do we do?" Sydney asked.

"I could back up and try another way or we could go out and see if we can move them out of the way." Sam responded as he turned the bus off and sat there staring at the mess in front of us.

"Hey I don't know if this helps or not, but Wayne's group and I had a system we were using when we went out for supplies." Aaron said.

"What would that be?" Sam asked.

"We'd spray paint a green x on doors of buildings that were clear and a red x on buildings that had Red Eyes in them. I could go through and start marking the cars that are clear or ones that have bodies in them." Aaron suggested.

"We don't have paint." Sam said.

"I have cans in my bag." Aaron responded.

"You know it's not a bad idea. That way if the kids go out they know which cars to stay away from." Sydney agreed, patting Aaron on the shoulder.

I followed Aaron outside and watched as he started going from vehicle to vehicle. He was putting x's on the windows. After I'd been watching him for a while he came back over to the bus.

"Do you want to help me with this?" he asked, I noticed at least a couple cars have keys in them we can mark those cars with two x's."

"Yeah I'll help." I agreed and he handed me two cans of spray paint.

Soon we had every vehicle marked, they were nineteen altogether. Eleven of them had red x's and eight had green ones. We were heading back to Sam when we started hearing a muffled thumping noise. As we got closer to the noise we started hearing a voice.

"Is someone out there? Please help me?" the voice called out.

"Where are you?" Aaron called back.

"The trunk of the red Neon." The voice answered.

"Try the door, if its unlocked pop the trunk and stay back till I say it's safe." Aaron directed me as we stood by the Neon.

I walked to the front of the car and did as I was told. The door was unlocked so I popped the trunk. I looked at Aaron and he nodded at me.

"Come on over Ash, I may need your help." Aaron said as he knelt down looking into the trunk. I joined him and found there was a black boy now sitting up.

"Thank you," he said to us as he accepted the water Aaron offered him.

"What's your name and why were you in the trunk?" Aaron asked him as soon as he stopped drinking.

"Micah. Micah Hender. My dad locked me in here." Micah explained to us, "We were trying to get to Phoenix."

"Why?" Aaron asked.

"We were going to find my mom and sisters but we ran into this road block." Micah said, "Dad tried to turn around but the people behind us panicked. They left their vehicles when a group of monsters came through. I heard screaming."

"How did you end up in the truck?" I asked.

"Dad thought I'd be safe in the trunk and had me get in with water and protein bars. He left me the key so I could get out if he didn't make it back but the batteries are dead so it wouldn't work." Micah answered.

"How long have you been in there?" I asked him, noticing that there were quite a few empty wrappers and bottles and there was the smell of urine.

"I don't know. Three days maybe. I ran out of water last night and the protein bars yesterday." Micah answered as he tried to lift himself out of the trunk, Aaron caught him before he fell.

"Whoa let's get you cleaned up and in some clean clothes dude, no offence but you reek." Aaron told him. Micah just nodded.

"Yeah, let's see if you come out looking your best after being stuck in a car trunk for three days." He said as he let Aaron help him back to the bus.

Sam met us about halfway and went to the other side to help Micah. We got him on the bus and Sam took him into the bathroom where he helped Micah shower. We all gathered in the living room to wait for them to come out. I quickly explained to everyone what Micah had told us and where we had found him.

"It's good we grabbed those clothes when we did. I hope something fits him." Daisy said. She had already grabbed a whole pile of clothes for Micah to try on. She even had shoes; I didn't remember us grabbing shoes, but of course she was the shoe girl.

Sam opened the bathroom door and before he could even ask Daisy was pushing the clothes towards him. Sam smiled at her and nodded then disappeared back into the bathroom. A few minutes later they came out. Micah was leaning on Sam as his legs shook on the walk over to the couch. Micah seemed to find clothes that fit; he was now wearing blue jeans and a plain white T-shirt.

"Thank you for the clothes." He said as Sam helped him to the couch.

"No problem, you got lucky that we grabbed a bunch when we were stocking up at Wal-Mart the other day." Daisy told him.

"It's hard to think about how much was going on while I was sitting in that trunk." He said.

"Yeah, Ashlyn filled us in on what happened to you." Sawyer told him, "I'm Sawyer by the way."

"Nice to meet you." Micah told her.

"Okay, we will have plenty of time to get to know Micah after we figure out the cars outside." Sam cut in bringing us all back to the fact that we were stuck at the moment.

"Ash and I marked all the cars. Double x's for keys. Red equals bodies or gore while green is all clear." Aaron told Sam.

"Good, I want to get the cars off the road. We'll line up ones with keys for easy access on the side of the road. If someone else comes this way and needs a vehicle they can take one. I also don't want to take any supplies out of them as someone else may need them and we are pretty stocked up." Sam directed us.

We got to work. Sydney, Aaron and Sam moved cars with a red x on them while Daisy, Sawyer and I moved the green ones.

Sam found a tow rope in a truck that had keys. Aaron maneuvered a pickup truck around for us to attach the rope to pull the cars that did not have keys. Sam directed Aaron to get cars that would be easy to hot-wire, parked in a reachable area.

It took longer than it seemed like it should to get the road cleared off. Especially since we wanted to go back in the bus to talk to Micah.

"Looks like the only thing we really can't move is that semi-truck." Aaron said, "Even if it had keys it's wedged into that ditch."

He was pointing over to where the semi was. I looked over to see what he was talking about. I noticed that even though the trailer was straight on the road, the cab was in the ditch, we'd need a tow truck to move it.

"Well, the way looks clear enough to get the bus through and for anyone going this way to make it." Sam decided, "Let's load up and get out of here."

It was a relief to get back on to the bus. Daisy and I both laid down on the floor in the living room while Sawyer went and sat down next to Micah.

"How are your legs doing?" she asked him.

"Getting better. Tone said I should keep standing up and sitting back down to get them working normal again." He answered.

"That's good. How are you feeling other than that?" Sawyer asked.

"Pretty good. Tone got me some food to eat, not much so I wouldn't throw it all back up." Micah answered, "Sorry for the overshare but hell I got pulled in here covered in my own piss."

"Its fine, I'm just glad we found you." Sawyer said and patted his hand.

"I'm glad you guys found me too. Not just for the fact that I would have died but because if someone else had, they may not have been a good group." Micah said, babbling a little.

Sawyer had her head on Micah's shoulder. He was holding her hand, his thumb caressing hers.

They seemed to be comforting each other. They really seemed to like each other's company and were chatting easily with each other. It's the most I'd seen Sawyer interact with anyone since Marie turned crazed. Even less so since Jenny sacrificed herself.

It was good to see her opening up to someone, she was not someone who did well being withdrawn. Daisy poked my shoulder and when I looked at her she pointed to Micah and Sawyer. She mimicked kissing behind her hand where they couldn't see.

I ended up choking on my laughter as I wondered if she was right, if they were into each other that way.

"What are you laughing at?" Sawyer asked me as she nudged me with the tip of her shoe.

"Nothing, Daisy was just making faces." I answered and Daisy tried to look innocent.

"Hey boys, looks like we have teenagers actually acting like teenagers. We must be doing something right." Sydney called to Sam and Tone.

"Are we sure that's a good thing? If I remember correctly teenagers are troublemakers. I'm thinking we may have to make them walk the rest of the way, what do you think Sam?" Tone asked.

"I don't know Tone; how much trouble are we talking here?" Sam asked.

"Ha ha you all are so funny." Daisy said as she threw a pillow that had fallen off the couch at Sydney.

"I'm hit!" Sydney called as she pretended to fall over.

"Hey Ash, I wonder if she's ticklish?" Daisy said to me and winked.

"Let's find out." I said as we both jumped over and grabbed Sydney. She squealed. She wiggled until she managed to escape us. Sydney crawled away. Micah laughed drawing our attention to him. His dark skin couldn't hide his blush. Angela, Thomas, and Axel were all laughing in the hallway. For a moment everyone on the bus forgot about the chaos we were escaping from.

Chapter Eight

The bus jolted to a stop. I looked out the window but everything looked clear. I watched Sam wondering what had happened now as he stood and looked back at us all.

"I thought we'd stop for lunch and as long as everyone stays close to the bus I think we can eat outside." He told us, "You might like the view."

"View? Where are we?" Sawyer asked as she turned to look out the window. Outside there was a lake and covered picnic tables.

"We're at Ashurst Lake." Sam said as he smiled. I looked out the window again focusing on what was there instead of looking for danger. I could see the rocky shoreline surrounding the calm water of the small lake.

"We can eat outside? Is it safe?" Axel asked as he practically had his face plastered to the window of the bus gazing at the water.

"Yeah I managed to get us right next to a table and as long as we all stay close we can all get away if we have to." Sam said. It was obvious he was getting the reaction he had been hoping for.

Given the option to get off the bus had all of us run over each other trying to get off the bus. We all wanted to see how close to the water we were and if we'd be able to play in it. Sydney stayed on the bus to make lunch with Tone, while Sam and Aaron came with us. Aaron was the first one to get into the water. Sam had parked close so the water was within the limits he set for us.

"Aaron, make sure you're keeping an eye on all our kids here." Sam said as he sat at the picnic table with Thomas.

Angela was walking with Axel near the water. There was squealing when he leaned down and splashed her with the water. Angela retaliated by shoving him into the water but she didn't make it away before he grabbed her and she went in with him. They both came up sputtering and splashing each other.

Aaron snuck up on Daisy, Sawyer, and I with help from Micah. I saw dark arms wrap around Sawyer's waist at the same time I felt myself being lifted.

Sawyer screamed as she was dunked backwards into the water. Her feet still kicking at the air as they followed her down. My stomach dropped into my feet as I was thrown upwards. I was screaming as I hit the water.

I coughed and spit water as I came back up. Daisy was splashing water as she tried to ward Aaron off; she backed right into Micah and disappeared under the water.

It was perfect like nothing bad had happened and we were a family out at the lake having fun. The sky had only a few of those puffy white clouds.

"Do you see a bicycle?" Sawyer asked me as she pointed above us.

I followed her finger to the cloud she was pointing at. There were two almost perfect circles connected by a thin line and two 'T' shapes going up from the line.

"Yeah it does." I told her.

I watched as Aaron snuck up on Micah and jumped backwards with him. Micah just had time to bring his hand up to hold his nose before the water swallowed him. It was the perfect summer day. I had almost forgotten all about lunch when Sydney and Tone came off the bus with grilled chicken and salad.

"Hey kids, lunch!" Tone called out to get us to the table.

"Did he just call me a kid?" Aaron asked as we walked up to the table.

"Hey I saw you in the water and you know if the shoe fits." Tone told him as he passed him a plate to put his food on.

"I'm going to take it as a compliment." Aaron decided as he grabbed a piece of chicken and some salad off the serving plates.

Angela had set Thomas and herself up on the ground with a plate between them. She was trying to get him to eat some of the salad with the chicken he had already eaten half of. They were both laughing as she tried to trick him into taking another bite. She sometimes succeeded. They were cute together with their matching eyes and brown hair. If it weren't for the age gap they could have been twins.

Sydney's chicken came out amazing. I had no idea what she put on it, but I was hoping she'd make it again for us. Tone claimed he did the salad and it wasn't half bad.

"You know you guys never told us if you have anyone out there you're worried about."

Daisy pointed out as we all enjoyed the sunshine.

"Well I have a fiancé, Noah, but I couldn't get a hold of him or find him when everything went bad." Sydney told us.

"Do you think he'll find you?" I asked.

"I left a message at our apartment telling him where I was going and to join us. I keep hoping I'll see his car pull up behind us." She responded as she spun a ring around her finger. She caressed the stone without looking at it.

"What about you Tone?" Sawyer asked.

"My boyfriend, Jay was attacked. I didn't get to him in time." Tone answered. "The Red Eye ripped his throat clear out, he died in my arms. I keep thinking I have to stay alive for both of us. He would have kicked my ass if I let myself fall apart just because I miss him."

He looked towards the water. Tears were building up in his eyes.

"What was he like?" Micah asked Tone, "How long were you two together?"

"He was amazing and an artist. He loved to do wire work; in fact, he did the wire work on this necklace I'm wearing." Tone said as he held out the black stone held in vines of silver.

"What's the stone?" Micah asked. Tone looked down and traced the vines.

"It's onyx. To protect me. He was into all that gemstone magic stuff." Tone explained with a little smile pulling at his lips, "To hear him talk about why he put certain stones in certain pieces was like listening to someone write a song."

"How long were you together?" I asked.

"We'd been together three years. I was planning to ask him to marry me on his birthday. I even went and bought a ring with a lapis lazuli stone." Tone responded.

"What does lapis lazuli do?" Aaron asked.

"I picked it for its encouraging creativity values." Tone answered.

"That necklace is amazing. I wish we could have met him." I told Tone as I got up and hugged him. He hugged me back.

"What's Noah like, Sydney?" Sawyer asked.

"He's a lawyer but not the bull shit ones you see on TV that don't really care about their clients. He loves his job and really believes in making sure everyone has the fairness they deserve. He trusts people, makes him a great lawyer." She said, "We were planning a spring wedding followed by a honeymoon in Europe. Now I guess we'll see if we find each other again."

She spun her ring around her finger again.

"Thomas!" Angela's voice was shrill as she called for her little brother. The panic in her voice made my heart pound. All of us moved at once to where she was standing, crying.

"Angela what happened?" Axel asked her before anyone had a chance to speak.

"I can't find Thomas. I just went to use the bathroom and when I came back he was gone." She cried, "Did anyone see where he went?"

"Don't worry hon, we'll find him." Sydney said as she took Angela's hand.

"Okay we're doing this in groups." Sam said.

"Sounds good what do you want us to do, boss?" Tone asked.

"Sydney, take Angela back on the bus. Axel, you're with me, Tone you've got Sawyer and Micah, and Aaron you have Ashlyn and Daisy. Spread out but stay within shouting distance and let's find Thomas." Sam commanded everyone, taking charge of the situation.

"I want to help." Angela cried. "He's my brother."

"Sam I've got her, we'll look too. I don't think she'll be able to sit on the bus until we find Thomas." Sydney told him.

Sam gave her a look that I couldn't read but I think he was worried how Angela would react.

"Okay, keep her close." Sam said looking hard at Sydney. She nodded at the look Sam was giving her.

We spread out, all of us combing through the tall grass close to the water to see if he was hiding there. Aaron was even scanning the water to see if he had fallen in.

"He can swim." Angela told him when she saw where he was looking. She was still holding Sydney's hand.

"Just making sure we're not worrying and all he did was take a swim." Aaron responded to her without missing a beat.

We were looking under the bus when I noticed a path on the other side of the road that went into the trees. I didn't think he could have made it there without us noticing but we went down it anyway.

We were all calling out his name when we heard the screaming. Sydney couldn't keep hold of Angela as she broke free and ran towards the noise. We all followed, running. Tone and Sydney had their guns drawn; I couldn't see Sam to see if he did as well.

We broke through to a clearing and there was Thomas. A Red Eye had his foot and he was trying to kick himself free but the creature was too strong. Before anyone could get a clear shot on the Red Eye, it took a bite out of his calf.

There was a lot of blood followed by the sound of a gun going off. I don't know who shot it, all I saw was Angela screaming and grabbing Thomas.

"We have to get him to the bus; maybe we can stop the infection." Sam called out and Aaron scooped Thomas up as he ran for the bus, all of us were on his heels.

I didn't realize I was crying till we were all back on the bus and a tear fell on my hand.

"Aaron I need you to hold him on your lap we're going to clean the bite with alcohol than I'm going to cauterize it. Sydney get something heated up that will cover the whole bite at once I don't want to have to do this to him more than once." Sam told us.

Sydney grabbed a metal spatula and an oven mitt as Sam opened a bottle of Vodka and poured onto the bite.

Thomas screamed and tried to get away.

Aaron held on to him until he exhausted himself and couldn't fight.

Sydney came back holding the spatula that was hot enough for the metal to be red. She handed it to Sam careful not to burn him in the process.

Sam immediately pressed the metal to Thomas's leg and it did cover the whole bite on his small leg.

The scream that came out of the small boy was more animal than human and didn't stop until he passed out. Angela was crying and hanging onto Sydney.

Sam spread some ointment onto the burned flesh and wrapped it up with an ace bandage. He looked ragged as he picked up Thomas from Aaron's lap and brought him out to one of the couches. He sat down and placed Thomas's head on his lap.

"Now what?" Angela asked as she picked up her brother's legs and laid them across her lap. She was careful not to touch the bandaged wound.

"Now we wait till he wakes up. We keep that bandage clean and keep out any infection and we watch him for symptoms." Sam answered as he squeezed Angela's hand, "We've done all we can here. When we get to Paradis Roulette my nephew has a fully-staffed hospital. He'll have them do everything they can."

"Will he be ok?" Angela asked again, she was watching her brother's sleeping face.

"I hope so but we won't know anything right away." Sam responded. "Tone, you good to drive? We have to get moving."

"Yeah I got it." Tone said and walked back to the driver's seat. Sydney joined him in the passenger seat while Aaron stayed with us. He had both Daisy and my hand; I hadn't even realized I had reached out to him when he had gotten up from holding Thomas.

Thomas slept even after we got to where Tone decided to park the bus for the night. Sydney was already asleep in her seat and Tone reclined his. Sam was still sitting with Thomas lying on his lap watching his every breath. Angela had fallen asleep where she was sitting on the couch; she was holding one of Thomas's hands.

"All of you should sleep there's nothing more we can do for him tonight." Sam told us and we all listened to him.

Daisy didn't want to sleep alone so she had Sawyer and I join her in her bedroom. Axel and Micah took the room Sawyer and I had been sharing while Aaron went to Sydney's room. None of us said much to each other. The bus that had been filled with laughter was silent. We all went to sleep hoping Thomas would be awake in the morning.

Chapter Nine

The morning came and was just as grey as our moods.

Everyone was edgy, eyes darting over to Thomas and back to the cereal we were eating. Thomas was still asleep on the couch. Sam was no longer sitting with him; he was up with Tone in the front of the bus with the door closed. Sydney was trying to cheer us up, but it was impossible with Angela sitting there. She had tears leaking constantly out of her eyes.

"All of you are going to upset Thomas when he wakes up." Sydney said as a last effort "He's going to think he has no chance."

"Does he really have a chance?" Angela asked, talking for the first time since we found Thomas.

"Yes, Sam did everything he could and I think it was his best chance." Sydney said to her as she crouched down in front of her and took both her hands.

"If I would have brought him with me he wouldn't have been bit." Angela sniffled.

"No honey it wasn't your fault, we all should have been paying more attention. He's young and curious." Sydney told her.

I didn't realize how much she was blaming herself for what had happened. She thought Thomas was her responsibility with their parents being gone.

"Will he get better?" Angela asked not quite voicing what we were all worried about—would he turn?

"First he has to wake up and then we will see." Sydney told her.

We all found a place to sit near Thomas as the bus started rolling again. Daisy coaxed Angela and Axel into playing a game of Monopoly.

Sawyer sat whispering with Micah. I was sitting near Thomas's head and fiddling with his hair a bit as I watched Daisy play with Angela and Axel. They both seemed to be letting Angela win. She was somber, even when she smiled or laughed.

Thomas finally started to wake up and at the first moan Sydney was there. She got him up slowly and held him. He seemed groggy but smiled when his eyes found Angela. She was up and by his side.

"Hey sleepy head." Angela said to him as she ruffled his hair, "How're you feeling?"

"My leg hurts. Did I get bit?" Thomas responded and went to touch his leg but Sydney grabbed his hand.

"No sweetie you can't touch that. Do you remember what Sam did to help stop the infection?" Sydney asked him as she rubbed his palm in her hand.

"Yeah it hurt a lot." Thomas said "Am I going to be a Red Eye?"

"No sweetie we wouldn't let that happen to you." Sydney said and he hugged her.

Thomas and Angela both hugged Sydney. Angela wanted to know what she could do to help keep the bandage on Thomas's leg clean. It was hard to believe that she was only fourteen, she acted a lot older. I was wondering how much time Thomas and her had spent alone, neither one would talk about their parents.

Neither Sam nor Tone came back to the main part of the bus. Sydney went up and talked to them a bit but she wouldn't say anything to us when she returned. She gave Thomas some sort of pain pills to help keep the pain in his leg in check so he could play with Angela and Axel.

They had found chutes and ladders in the pile of games. Apparently it was Thomas's favorite; he lit up when he saw it. Of course they were letting him win. Every time he won, he'd stand up and do a victory dance that looked a lot like the chicken dance.

Thomas barely made it through lunch before he fell asleep again. Angela was worried but Sydney told her it was normal; he was healing from a traumatic experience. Angela got Thomas to their room and left the door open so if he woke up we would all know.

The bus rocked like it hit a pot hole and came to an abrupt stop. Angela ran back to the room to check that Thomas hadn't been thrown from the bed. She came back and stood next to Axel as we waited for Sam or Tone to come and tell us what had happened.

"Is everyone okay?" Sam asked as he opened the door, he looked relieved to see us all standing there.

"I think so. Did we hit something?" Sydney asked.

"Not something. Someone." Sam answered, his hands were shaking, "I tried to stop but they were in front of us too fast. I don't know if—"

"We should go check the body and bury him." Tone added as he came into the living room.

"Is it safe out there? What if he was being chased?" Sydney asked as she wrapped her arms around Angela and Axel, both standing closest to her.

"That is one point. If we just leave, is that going to be something we can live with?" Sam asked as he sat down.

"Any chance he survived?" Sawyer asked and I noticed she was holding Micah's hand.

"No. I don't know how much this bus weighs but the tires went over him." Tone answered.

"My vote's for leaving." Sydney said. "Not to sound heartless but we do have everyone else on this bus to think of. Plus, if he was running from something we are risking getting ourselves hurt or killed. For someone we can't help, someone who is already dead."

"I have to say I agree but since we are all in this together I didn't want to make the call." Sam said as he stood up and headed back to the driver's seat. He didn't shut the door as he started the bus back up and got us moving.

I remembered news stories about hit and runs. How horrible they were. Now everything was different. There were risks now that no one would have dreamed to worry about before. I didn't know how I felt; I wanted to know who he was. But I didn't want to see him either.

I didn't realize I was crying until Aaron came and sat by me. He didn't say anything just hugged me and put his chin on my head.

"It's okay to be upset." He said to me.

"Was it right to leave him? Is this what the world is now?" I asked as I hugged him.

"I don't know if it was right but it was safest for everyone on this bus. You remember now that other people made the decision." He said.

"But I feel relief that they made that decision, what does that say about me?" I asked him as I pulled away and looked into his blue-green eyes.

"It says that you're scared of what this world has turned into. Which you shouldn't be ashamed of, I'm scared too. That's why I did what Wayne said to do; I thought I was safe with him." Aaron told me, "I'll do better than he did. As long as I'm here I will look after you and everyone else the best I can and I will die trying to keep you all safe."

"Thank you Aaron." I responded.

"The way I see it we have a lot in common, we should look out for each other." Aaron said as he kissed my forehead, "I miss Emily. I had always wanted a little sister when she was born."

"Really?" I asked smiling, "My sister used to say I was a pain in the ass."

"Yeah, she was too, but it looks like we have a whole big family now. I should've known all that hoping for a baby sister to protect when I was a kid would backfire." Aaron said, "Now I have more people to protect then I ever thought I would. It's scary since I failed to protect Emily."

"Guess you should be careful what you hope for." I said.

"But seriously, whenever you feel scared or alone, you come find me, got it?"

"I got it." I laid my head on his leg and he ran fingers through my hair till I fell asleep.

When I woke up, the bus had stopped and Aaron was still sitting but he was asleep. His hand was on my head. I tried to sit without waking him, but the second I moved he woke up. He smiled at me as he stretched, and ruffled my hair the same way I'd seen him do to Emily millions of times.

"Where are we?" He asked.

"Not sure." Sydney answered, "Sam and Tone said they needed to take a break from driving."

"How's the boy doing?" Aaron asked.

"He's awake again but he won't drink water yet." Sydney answered, "He seems pretty good other than that."

"Any sign of infection?" I asked.

"So far he's doing well. The skin around the bite isn't red and he seems like he's going to be okay. But it's only been a day." She said, "Now Aaron if you don't mind I'd like to borrow Ashlyn."

Aaron didn't say anything just nodded and ruffled my hair again.

"See you later Ash." Aaron said as he headed to the bathroom.

I followed Sydney to the kitchen where she was quiet for a while before she turned around and looked at me.

"How old are you?" she asked me.

"Seventeen." I answered "Why?"

"You know Aaron is way too old for you, right?" Sydney started.

"Too old for me?" I asked.

"Yes, the world's gone crazy but not that crazy." Sydney answered.

"Wait. What are you assuming he wants?" I asked.

"I don't know what he wants but it seems like he's getting closer to you." Sydney said.

"Yeah we're all getting closer. I was friends with his sister, remember? I've known him for years. Since we're like family now, I guess that makes you mom." I snapped at her.

"I forgot you knew him before this. We're like a family now? What does he call you?" she asked.

"Little sister, with Emily gone and him knowing me, he wants to protect me." I answered, "Why are you looking for bad in him? Isn't there enough bad in the world as it is right now? You guys let him stay. So when he starts to integrate with us, now you're worried about what his intentions are?" I was gripping the counter.

"You know what, you're right. He doesn't talk to me much so I don't know much about him. I see he hangs out with you a lot and I was worried that there was more going on." Sydney tried to explain herself.

"Shouldn't we be spending more time on worrying about Thomas than Aaron? I heard what you said about water and I remember those crazed in the Wal-Mart." I told her.

"The water may be nothing. It might be he is just a little boy and water has no sugar in it. He is drinking other liquids even when they are watered down." Sydney answered.

"Are you sure it's nothing to worry about? We don't know how fast a bite infects someone and he's so little." I said.

"Ashlyn, we don't know, so don't say anything, we don't want to upset Angela for no reason." She said. I nodded and walked away. I didn't want to join chutes and ladders, and Sawyer was cozied up to Micah on the couch. I wasn't sure what was really going on with them but I knew Sawyer would tell me if there was anything to tell. I ended up going to my room; I sat on the bed looking out the window at our surroundings. Aaron came in and joined me, he sat opposite of me.

"So what did Sydney think was going on?" Aaron asked.

"She thinks you want sex." I answered. His eyes darkened and he shook his head.

"Yup, people always think the worst." Aaron said, "You have to admit, it's kind of funny with everything else being shit. She's worried about my intentions. Hell, there's a whole world of crazy out there. Can you imagine Emily's reaction to that?"

"Yeah." I responded.

"Okay Ash what's up?" Aaron asked me, he was looking at me like my face would answer his question.

"We went into a Wal-Mart and were attacked by some crazed. They were afraid of water. Now Thomas won't drink water and he was bit. I'm worried. But you can't tell anyone I said anything." I answered. "They want to wait because Sydney thinks it could just be that he doesn't like plain water."

"Well then, I guess we'll just have to keep an eye on him and hope Sydney is right." Aaron said as he turned and looked out the window. "Looks like we're going to be moving soon, there in the trees do you see the Red Eyes?"

"How do you know they're Red Eyes from here?" I asked. I could see the people in the trees walking towards the bus.

"Look at how they walk." Aaron answered as we felt the bus come to life and the people got smaller as we pulled away. "Do you see how slow they're moving?"

I watched the group more closely. I noticed there was stiffness to the movement the group was making. They moved like marionettes.

"Okay, I see the movements are different. How could you tell that fast?" I asked.

"From all the hunting I did with Wayne and Emily. You learn to notice how things move." He answered as we watched Red Eyes disappear from view.

Chapter Ten

The smell of spaghetti and garlic bread drifted through the bus.

"Hope everyone likes SpaghettiO's and Texas toast." Sydney greeted as we followed our noses.

"Where's Thomas?" Sydney asked Angela.

"He refused to come out. He said that his head hurt and the light hurt his eyes." Angela answered as she tore off a piece of her toast and dipped it in the SpaghettiO's.

Aaron shot a look at me that said we definitely had to keep an eye on the boy, to keep the rest of our family safe. I noticed that Sydney was watching both Aaron and I, her eyes holding a warning.

"Did Thomas get some sleep Angela?" Sydney asked as Sam and Tone finally came out of the front of the bus to join us. They both looked grim.

"Yeah he slept all afternoon but he says his head hurts now and the light makes him cry." Angela answered as she kept eating. She didn't see the look that passed between Sam, Tone, and Sydney.

"Well, when you're done eating you can bring him some dinner. We'll give you some pain killers to give him, maybe that will help and he'll come out and play tomorrow." Sam told her.

"Yeah, he'll love having dinner in bed! It'll be just like when he got sick at home and mom would bring him all his meals in his room. She'd read him a story as he ate and he'd sleep." Angela told us, it was the most she had said about her parents so far.

There wasn't any real conversation between us through the rest of dinner. Sawyer and Micah were talking quietly together. Angela finished as quickly as she could. She disappeared back into the room, bringing Thomas food and pain killers. Daisy was trying to engage Axel in conversation but he kept staring at where Angela went. Aaron was sitting next to me, but we ate in silence.

"Listen up." Sam said breaking the shell we were all in.

"Yeah?" Sydney asked.

"We all need to talk about what we are going to do about Thomas. If his symptoms are not just from what happened to him and healing, then we have to be prepared for him turning." Sam responded as he looked around the room. Aaron looked at me.

"I thought he was getting better." Axel said, "That's what Sydney told Angela."

"He might be but some of the things he's doing right now are very similar to the symptoms the crazed showed." Tone answered.

"Then shouldn't Angela be out here to have a say in everything?" Axel asked, "It is her brother we are talking about and you lied to her."

"We didn't lie to her. We don't know what's going to happen and we don't want her to worry if it's nothing. It would be cruel to scare her." Sydney told him, trying to calm him down.

"You're talking about possibly having to kill her brother and you waited till she wasn't in the room to do so." Axel said through gritted teeth. Aaron walked over to stand in front of Axel.

"Look Axel, everyone wants Thomas to be fine, but we have to be prepared to protect all of us if he isn't." Aaron told Axel as he kneeled down to look him straight in the eyes.

"Can you honestly say you could kill Thomas?" Axel asked him.

"Yes. If it came to that. To protect the rest of us, I could pull the trigger." Aaron answered. Axel spit in his face.

"You wouldn't kill Thomas would you?" Angela cried. She had come out of the room without us hearing her. There was no telling how much she had heard but she had definitely heard what Aaron had just said.

"Sweetie we didn't want to worry you." Sydney answered.

"You said he was getting better." Angela said.

"We just want to be prepared in case we are wrong and he isn't getting better." Sydney said soothingly to her and tried to take her hand. Angela pulled away out of her reach.

"You're out here planning to kill my little brother. Are you even going to give him a chance or were you just waiting till I fell asleep?" Angela choked out between sobs. Her face was wet from the tears and I couldn't blame her, this must feel like a betrayal.

"We're not planning to kill your brother. We are planning on how to protect everybody if he's not getting better." Tone tried to talk to her.

"You are all just liars; you said we were safe here with you." Angela said as she threw the plate she was holding at Sydney, "I hate all of you!"

Angela stormed out of the room, stumbling and coughing and sobbing. She went into her room and slammed the door. The lock clicked. Choking sobbing sounds continued to carry through the bus. Sydney looked defeated. Axel looked guilty and hurt. Sam and Tone were whispering to each other. The rest just looked on, shocked.

"Okay everyone we need to get some sleep. We'll talk to Angela tomorrow and she'll understand what she walked into. For now, she won't hear anything we say." Sam said.

Daisy headed to her room with Axel on her heels. Through the open door we watched her hand him blankets and a pillow. He set up a place for himself on the floor at the foot of her bed, which looked a lot like a nest.

"You got him?" Sydney asked her. Daisy nodded as she shut the bedroom door.

"Ashlyn, do you mind Micah sleeping in our room tonight? He'll sleep on the floor." Sawyer asked me.

"No that's fine." I answered.

"Hey you should get sleep too; we'll figure this out tomorrow." Aaron told me.

"Will it be okay?" I whispered to him as I hugged him.

"I don't know, but we'll get through it." He whispered back.

I followed Sawyer and Micah into our room where he already had a spot made up on the floor and she was crawling into bed. I followed her and Micah turned off the light.

I didn't think I would sleep but as soon as I lay down I was out.

The room was still dim but bathed in pink when Aaron shook me awake.

"Shh." He said motioning to Sawyer and Micah. Sometime during the night Sawyer had moved off the bed and was cuddled up with Micah. I followed Aaron out of the room and he led me outside.

"What are we doing?" I asked him as we walked to the front of the bus.

"Look, I've been thinking. I mean, things go bad, yeah, sure. Some of that bad was yesterday. We do what we gotta do, but it's like you have to remember the good too." He told me as he pointed to the sky where the sun was just beginning to peek out from behind the mountain. Within minutes the sky was pink chased by orange. Aaron was right, it was beautiful and I had forgotten that things could be this perfect.

We were still standing out there watching the sky when Sydney came running out.

"Are they with you?" She asked, sounding panicked.

"Who?" Aaron asked.

"Angela and Thomas." She answered, looking around the other side of the bus.

"No we haven't seen them." I answered.

"They're gone. They aren't in their room and their stuff is gone." Sydney said as Sam and Tone came up to us.

"Any luck?" Tone asked as soon as he saw Sydney.

"No they haven't seen them. Where could they be?" She responded.

"They can't be far, we'll find them. Angela probably panicked and thought she was saving him. The problem is if he's really turning, then she's in very serious danger." Sam said more to himself as he placed a hand on his hat.

"We can't have everyone out looking for them; someone needs to stay with the bus and the kids that stay." Sydney said.

"You're right Sydney; would you be willing to stay with the kids and keep everyone calm?" Tone asked her. She looked at him and nodded as his words sunk in.

"Yes, I can do that." She agreed, "I'll go start breakfast."

"Tone you're with me, Aaron would you be okay on your own?" Sam asked.

"He won't be on his own, I'll go." I told him. Sam looked like he was going to argue with me but Aaron cut him off.

"Don't worry I won't let anything happen to her." He said.

"Okay we'll head back the way we came, how about you both head the way we're going." Sam agreed even though he didn't look happy about it.

Chapter Eleven

Both our little groups headed off in opposite directions. We had all grabbed some water to take with us. Everyone else on the bus was still asleep and Sam was hoping we would find Angela and Thomas before they woke up. Aaron was walking more in the ditch when we found the first foot prints.

"I think they went this way, do you see where there's mud?" Aaron asked and there on the ground by his feet were two sets of footprints.

"Looks like they stayed in the ditch near the road. Should we get the others?" I asked.

"Yeah but we'd have to run to get them, you up for that?" Aaron responded and I nodded.

We ran back towards the bus. We could see Sam and Tone on the road up ahead, we didn't want to yell and attract any attention.

"Did you find something already?" Sam asked as soon as we caught up with them.

"Yup, there's prints in the mud, they're small." Aaron told him.

We headed back to where we saw the footprints with Sam and Tone following us. Nobody said anything when Aaron showed them the prints. We started following the trail. It turned out that Aaron's hunting skills had taught him how to track. He was picking up the trail when I thought there wasn't one.

We had been walking for quite a while steadily heading further into the woods when we came across an RV. We stopped and watched it for a while, but there didn't seem to be anything going on around it. No one coming out or walking around and there wasn't any noise coming from inside.

"Do you think it's abandoned?" Aaron asked.

"Maybe or whoever's in there is still asleep." Sam answered, still scanning the area.

"The trail heads towards the RV. Maybe they got lucky and found it abandoned. It would have given them shelter for the night since it seems she snuck him out as soon as we were all asleep." Aaron said, "We haven't seen any movement, I think we should check inside."

"Looks like that may be what happened." Tone agreed, "Ashlyn stay here."

"No she comes. She'll stay behind me but we're not leaving her anywhere." Aaron said and Tone just shrugged.

We moved quietly up to the RV. There wasn't any noise. Sam looked into the windows but they were all blocked. He tried the door and it opened easily and swung open. As soon as the light streamed in we saw the blood.

Following the trail, we saw Angela laying on the floor under a table, Thomas was sitting on her. He was covered in blood and when he turned to us his eyes were red. I could feel the tears falling from my eyes. Most of Angela's body was covered in blood. I could see her stomach was torn open and most of her innards were thrown around half eaten.

Thomas was growling at us as he started to move towards us, forgetting Angela. I never saw Tone raise his gun, but I heard it go off and then Thomas was on the floor, a hole in his forehead. He looked so small.

"Will she come back?" I asked looking back to Angela.

"No, look at her head. Its angled wrong, it looks like she hit it when he attacked her. You can see where he dug into the wound." Aaron told me gently. Sam was going into the RV.

"What are you doing?" Tone asked him.

"Seeing if there are blankets we can carry them in. I want to bring them back to the bus and bury them. Everyone will want to know what happened and say goodbye." Sam answered as he vanished and returned with two blankets.

I thought it was lucky that the blankets were a deep brown, they wouldn't show the blood. Sam very carefully wrapped both the bodies. He handed Angela to Tone, and carried Thomas himself.

"I want you two to go ahead and tell Sydney what happened and what we're doing. Let her tell the others." Sam said as he came out with the bundle that was all left of little Thomas.

"You heard him Ash. Come on I've got you." Aaron said as he grabbed my hand.

I followed Aaron mostly by his grip on my hand. I wasn't seeing anything around me. All I could see was Thomas's face, with those Red Eyes, and all of Angela's blood, it kept replaying. Aaron periodically squeezed my hand in an attempt to reassure me. I didn't even notice when we walked up to the bus. Aaron got me on and sat me down at the table.

"What happened? Is she okay?" Sydney asked.

"No she's not. We found Angela and Thomas but it's not good." Aaron said.

"How not good?" Sydney asked.

"Thomas turned. Tone had to shoot him. Sam and Tone are carrying the bodies back so we can give them a funeral." Aaron answered.

"What about Angela?" Sydney asked her hand was resting at the base of her throat.

Aaron shook his head.

"Oh God." Sydney said.

"Yeah, Sam said to let you tell the others." Aaron answered as the others were starting to come out of the rooms.

"Tell us what?" Axel asked.

"Kids, gather round and sit down." Sydney started and waited till everyone was seated.

"What's going on?" Sawyer asked.

"It looks like Angela took off last night with Thomas. We found them but we were too late." Sydney answered, "Tone and Sam are on their way back with their bodies, we're going to bury them. I want all of you to be prepared for a funeral."

"This is all your fault." Axel shot at Sydney as he started to cry, he let Daisy hold him but his eyes were shooting venom at Sydney. "If you would have told her the truth she'd be alive."

"Shhh, Axel we don't know that she may have panicked sooner and it wouldn't have ended any different." Daisy told him as she hugged him and he held on to her.

Everything around me seemed to be happening far away or to someone else. I didn't even realize Aaron had his arm around me.

"You're going to be okay, Ash." He whispered to me.

I noticed that he wasn't saying that everything would be okay, just that I would be.

I looked around the table at everyone and could see the shock on their faces as the tears fell.

"Will we all be okay?" I whispered to Aaron. He kissed my forehead.

"I think we'll all make it through this, once the shock wears off and we're back on the road." Aaron whispered back.

Sydney was making her way around the bus checking on everyone. It seemed that was how she was dealing; she was trying to take care of everyone else.

Axel still wouldn't talk to her and he wouldn't look at her. I was sure he'd forgive her once he thought about what had happened.

When Sydney came around to me, Aaron told her that he had me.

"You sure?" Sydney asked him.

"Yeah, I saw what she saw, I got her. She'll be okay." Aaron said. Sydney looked up out of the window and I heard her sigh before she turned to everyone.

"Sam and Tone are back." She said "Let's go help them and say our goodbyes."

No one responded but everyone got up and filed off the bus. There was more crying when they saw the blankets. Sydney came off the bus with shovels and I saw Axel take one from her. He went and started digging a hole as Sam dug another.

Chapter Twelve

The holes were dug.

Sam was gently laying both Angela and Thomas into them. We all threw a handful of dirt onto them and said our silent goodbyes. Sam and Axel worked together to fill in the graves. Axel was shaking with every shovelful of dirt he placed over Angela.

"I don't know which religion they were so I'm not going to quote the bible here." Sam started, "We are all here today to say goodbye to Angela and Thomas. Both were too young to be taken away but we'll remember them always."

No one said 'Amen' or anything. Mostly everyone kept their heads down, saying whatever silent prayers that would send Angela and Thomas on their way.

We all stood there for a while before Sam started tapping us on the shoulder and sending us back onto the bus. He stood next to Axel for a few minutes before he did the same. Sam kept his arm over Axel's shoulders; it looked like that was the only thing propelling him back onto the bus.

Axel didn't even look at any of us, he went straight to the room Angela and Thomas had shared and shut the door.

"He'll be okay, just give him some time." Sam told everyone as he headed to the driver's seat followed by Tone.

"How's everyone else holding up?" Sydney asked as she looked around the bus.

No one answered her, she got a few nods or shrugs but we were all silent.

Everyone found a place to sit and was just taking comfort in the silence. We had all forgotten how bad things could be. We were in our own little bubble of safety on the bus, which kept us moving away from most of the bad things going on.

The horror hadn't touched us as much as it could have without our bubble as we headed to our destination. Losing both Angela and Thomas left us drained. I sat by Aaron and watched everyone else on the bus for a while.

"How're you holding up?" He asked me.

"I don't know." I answered, looking at him.

"Maybe Tone was right and you should have stayed back. Then you wouldn't have seen all that in the RV." Aaron said as he rubbed his temple.

"You know I would have gone anyway. I would have been sneaking and who knows what would have happened then." I told him, "What I saw isn't your fault. I keep thinking if we would have found them sooner maybe Angela would still be alive."

"Don't take me wrong, but maybe it is better this way. I mean how would Angela have dealt with losing Thomas?" Aaron said.

"There is that." I said.

"I don't want to sound like I don't care because I do. I just picture them somewhere together. Where none of this is happening and they are safe, maybe with their parents." Aaron continued.

"That is a nice thought." I agreed, "I like to think that they are someplace safe and happy. Maybe they'll even watch over us wherever they are."

"Like our very own guardian angels?" Aaron asked.

"I guess." I answered, "I just wish Axel wasn't locking himself away from everyone right now."

"He'll be fine. I think he had a crush on Angela and now she's gone." Aaron said, "He'll come out when he's ready to face everyone."

Sydney passed out peanut butter and jelly sandwiches to everyone. Axel had come out of the room that he claimed as his now, but he wasn't talking to anyone.

He had the chutes and ladders game in his lap and he was staring at it. He was barely eating his sandwich. Daisy was sitting near him. He wouldn't even let her get too close.

He may have stayed in the room, but he was shutting all of us out. He ate about half his sandwich before he got up to return to his room, he took chutes and ladders with him. As soon as his door closed, Daisy came and sat by Aaron and me.

"Has Axel said anything to you?" I asked her.

"No, but I didn't really think he would. He got close to Angela based on them both losing their parents." Daisy answered.

"That makes sense, bonding with someone who's lost what you have." Aaron said as he looked at me. We had bonded over the loss of our siblings.

Sam stopped the bus and when we looked outside we saw we were parked at a gas pump.

"We're fueling up and heading out again." He called back. Tone and Sam started to get off the bus, "Everyone stay on the bus."

It was a quick stop. We watched Sam run into the store and came out with no problems while Tone was filling the tank up. Sam stood guard as Tone stood with the pump. As soon as the tank was filled, they both got on the bus and we started to pull away.

"Not going to turn the pump off?" Sydney asked.

"No, make it easier for anyone else who needs to fill up, we left a note on the pump telling them it was on as well." Sam responded.

"Where to next?" Tone asked.

"There's a junk yard near here, we're going to park there tonight. There's a fence around it that should keep the Red Eyes away from us." Sam said, "We'll just have to deal with whatever is inside the fence."

"Why are we worried about keeping Red Eyes out? We haven't been worried about that any of the times we parked on the road." Sydney asked.

"We've passed whole hordes of Red Eyes so far. None of them seem to be following us but all it will take is them turning and following us.

They could overtake the bus; a fence will help."
Tone answered.

"There's no need to scare everyone Tone.
We've all been through enough today. Without
being worried that we can't sleep without being
killed." Sydney snapped at Tone.

"Well, you asked and last time we decided
to keep secrets we ended up burying two kids."
Tone snapped back. It was the first time we'd
heard them be anything but completely
supportive of what the other had said.

Sydney looked like she was taken back. I
knew in that moment she had made the call to
keep all of us in the dark about what was going
on with Thomas. She didn't say anything just
walked back to her room and shut the door.

"You didn't have to be so hard on her." Sam
said to Tone.

"I know but I feel like if we would have been
honest with Angela she wouldn't have snuck off.
We wouldn't have had to bury both of them."
Tone responded, "I just hope she was out or
dead when he started to eat her."

"I think she was already dead. She probably
fell and hit her head when he lunged at her. I
doubt she ever even felt a thing." Sam said. Tone
nodded but didn't respond.

The atmosphere was tense. We had lost people and no one had been prepared for it. It was still quiet when we pulled up to the junkyard. Sam and Tone went out to get the gate open and scout what we were going to be facing.

Sydney still hadn't come back out, so Aaron got behind the wheel and watched for either Tone or Sam to come back. He started the bus as Sam waved him through the gate, as soon as the bus was past the gate, he closed it. Tone waved the bus forward leading us to the spot Sam and he had found for us to park.

It was weird seeing piles of cars on either side of us blocking off anything else. It was creepy, like driving right into a horror movie.

Aaron parked the bus where Tone directed and shut it down. Neither Sam nor Tone got back on yet though.

"Don't look so worried Ash. They scouted the area otherwise they wouldn't have waved us in." Aaron told me.

"Yeah well then where are they?" I asked wondering what would be keeping both Sam and Tone outside.

It was still early evening so we had enough light to see outside but there was no sign of the two being around the bus.

"Probably making sure everything is secure. Double checking that we will be safe. You know they both take the safety of this group very seriously." Aaron said as he watched me, "We'll stay put till they come back."

Sydney still hadn't come out of her room, but Axel did. He was sitting with Micah and they were talking. I couldn't hear what they were saying but it was good to see Axel interacting with someone.

"Well look at that." Aaron said smiling as he pointed towards Micah and Axel.

"Yeah I think he'll be okay." I said as we watched the two boys bond over whatever they were talking about. Sawyer came out and her eyes searched for Micah instantly.

She gave them space when she saw Axel sitting there talking to him. Sawyer smiled as she watched them. I was watching her and I remembered seeing her give the same look to Josh right after she met him.

It was good seeing her eyes light up again. They'd been shadowed since she saw Josh at the hospital attacking the nurse and it got worse when we lost Jenny.

"Hey." She said to me as she came over and bumped her hip into mine.

"Hey back." I told her wrapping my arm around her waist.

"Hey, now is there something I should know?" Micah called to us making Axel laugh.

"Oh, did she forget to mention that I'm her wife?" I asked and looked at Sawyer.

"Umm, no she did not mention that." Micah answered.

"Oh am I just not good enough to mention now?" I tried pouting at her but neither of us could keep a straight face.

"So is that a joke? Or...?" Micah asked looking between us. Sawyer tried to cover her laugh with a cough. I couldn't stop the giggle that bubbled up.

"You're both dorks." Micah told us. He smiled as he rolled his grey eyes. He wrapped his arm around Sawyer.

"Well now that's a sound for sore ears." Sam said as he climbed back into the bus followed by Tone. "You hear this Tone?"

"Yeah, great sound to come home to." Tone said, "What do you think we missed?"

"Well apparently Miss Sawyer here is seeing Micah but forgot to mention she was Ash's Mrs." Aaron said.

"Well Micah, looks like you'll have to learn to share." Tone said without missing a beat.

"Oh...Micah, good luck man." Aaron joked as Sam stood there, a small smile crawling onto his face.

"It's good that we all find times to laugh and enjoy that we are all alive. Bad things are going to happen and they will keep happening." Sam said, "We have each other so try to remember good things, help each other through the bad."

"He's right. If we let the bad in this world take us over, we won't survive." Tone agreed.

"Does that mean we should invade Sydney's room and drag her out?" Daisy asked. Tone looked towards Sydney's door.

"No I should be the one to go and talk to her. I shouldn't have said what I did to her; she thought she was doing the right thing." Tone decided and headed to her room. He knocked but she didn't answer. That didn't stop Tone; he walked in and shut the door behind him.

"I think he's brave." Aaron said to no one in particular.

"I think you might be right." Sam agreed.

"Why?" Axel asked looking back to Sydney's door.

"It's best you learn this lesson young son. An upset woman is a lot like a bear. If they've locked themselves away like Sydney did, you're entering their lair." Sam told him. Axel looked at him for a few minutes while he processed the information.

"Well it's a good sign that we don't hear screaming or things being thrown." Aaron said and shrugged, "Maybe she'll let him keep his limbs."

"Should someone check on them to make sure?" Axel asked as he turned his attention to Aaron. Sam laughed as he shook his head.

Tone came out of Sydney's room limping and holding his hand. All of us fell silent wondering what had happened to him.

"It was a battle but she said she'll come out." Tone said as he collapsed onto the couch. He threw his arm over his eyes and let out a moan.

"Are you okay?" Axel asked as he got up and crouched by Tone.

"Have you ever braved dealing with an upset woman?" Tone asked lifting his arms off one of his eyes.

"No." Axel answered, "Can I get you anything?"

Tone didn't answer. Instead Sydney snuck up behind Axel and grabbed him in a bear hug causing him to scream in surprise. Tone sat up laughing.

"Sorry kid it was you or me." Tone apologized through his laughter.

"You tricked me!" Axel accused as Sydney put him down.

"Yes he did." Sydney said as she turned Axel to look at her. "I wanted to tell you I'm sorry. I should have told everyone what I was suspecting."

"Okay, but no more secrets" Axel said as he hugged her. "As Sam told us we have to hold on to each other and keep reminding each other that we're still here. There's still some good in the world."

"Well I didn't quite use those words, but yeah." Sam said as Sydney smiled and hugged him back.

"What's for dinner?" She asked as she looked at Sam.

"Wait, I never said I was cooking." Sam said as he looked at Sydney.

"Oh I know. I just threw you under the bus." She said, "Now who's up for a game?"

Chapter Thirteen

We were playing Clue. We had broken into teams of two so everyone could play.

Sam worked in the kitchen. The aroma of cooking burgers, potatoes, and corn drifted in the air. Tone had partnered with Daisy and they were playing as Mr. Green because of Daisy's hair. Sydney and Axel were a team playing as Miss Scarlet. Sawyer and Micah had teamed up and chosen Professor Plum. Aaron was my partner and we were Mrs. Peacock.

"Okay so we think it was Mrs. White in the Ballroom with the Revolver." Sawyer said as Micah moved the purple piece into the ballroom.

"Well we have Mrs. White and the Revolver." Tone said.

"And we have the Ballroom." Axel responded. Everyone marked off the new information on their paper before the next move. Next up was Sydney and Axel. They rolled and moved their red piece into the Kitchen.

"Okay so it was Mrs. Peacock in the Kitchen with the Rope." Axel said.

"Yeah well we have Peacock and the Rope." Micah responded.

"We have the Kitchen." Aaron said. He rolled as everyone filled in their papers. I moved our blue piece to the Billiard Room.

"So it was Green in the Billiard with the Knife." Aaron guessed.

"Nope we have the Billiard room." Micah responded.

"We have the knife and Mr. Green." Sydney added in. Next up we had Tone and Daisy rolling. They moved their green piece into the Hall.

"So Mustard in the Hall with the Candlestick?" Daisy asked.

"We have the Hall." Sawyer said.

"Candlestick." Aaron said.

"No one has Mustard?" Tone asked; everyone shook their heads. "One mystery solved."

"Now it's just a race to figure out the weapon and room." Daisy laughed. As Micah took the dice and rolled. Sawyer moved their piece to the Conservatory.

"Colonel Mustard, in the Conservatory, with the Wrench." Micah guessed.

"We have the Conservatory." Axel responded.

"Anyone have the wrench?" Sawyer asked. After everyone said they didn't Axel grabbed the dice to roll. They used their roll to move to the Study.

"How about Mustard, in the Study, with the Wrench?" Sydney asked. Nobody spoke up. Tone grabbed the packet in the middle of the board and pulled out the three cards in it. He revealed Colonel Mustard, the Wrench, and the Study.

"Nice you guys win." Tone congratulated Sydney and Axel with high fives.

"Just in time for dinner to be served." Sam called from the kitchen.

We quickly picked up the game and headed in to grab the food. Sam had laid everything out on the counters in a line. So we could grab a plate, buns, burger and go through to put everything we wanted on it.

It was an assembly line for dinner with the last things being fully loaded baked potatoes and the corn. We were all quieter as we ate, enjoying our meal and each other's company. Sam had even put on some music with an iPod and speakers. He didn't put it on very loud so it was just background noise.

"Wow Sam, I didn't know you knew how to work one of those." Tone said as he finished his potato.

"Very funny Tone." Sam responded, "Besides I'm not that old."

"Well I think it's time everyone got some sleep and we can get an early start tomorrow, get back onto the main road." Sydney told us, "Come on kids get a move on."

We all obeyed.

Micah went in to share the room with Axel; he kissed Sawyer as he walked by her. She giggled as she followed me back to our room. We didn't talk, just crawled into bed to sleep. I didn't realize how tired I was until I laid down.

The bed felt like heaven as soon as I got comfortable. Sawyer was asleep almost before her head was on her pillow. I looked up at the dark ceiling listening to her breathe.

I woke in the morning to the sun shining through the window and the bus was already moving. Sawyer was asleep when I left the room. It was surprising seeing that the living room was pretty much empty. Aaron was sitting on the couch reading a book. Tone was driving while Sam sat in the passenger seat navigating.

"Morning." Aaron greeted me, "Those two are boring."

"Hey now, we can hear you." Tone called back.

"Well that was the point." Aaron told him and winked at me, "There's some oatmeal on the counter. I made it about an hour or so ago."

"Thank you." I told him as I went to grab a bowl. I sat down next to him with my bowl and looked out of the window. In the distance there was black smoke rising to the sky.

"A fire?" I asked him as I nodded in the direction with my chin.

"Yeah, wasn't burning when we parked so it must have started last night." He answered, "See that smoke—how it's black."

"Yeah?" I answered.

"Means the fire is still burning, if you see the smoke turn white it means the fire is out." Aaron responded.

"Is it going to cause us any problem?" I asked.

"Hopefully not, but it is the reason Sam wanted to get an early start. Wanted to try to get ahead of it so there would be no chance of it cutting us off." Aaron answered as he picked his book back up. He was reading *The Enemy* by Charlie Higson.

"What's the book about?" I asked him.

"Pretty much zombie apocalypse." He answered.

"Really? With everything going on, that's what you choose to read?" I asked him.

"It sounded interesting and they have the whole series on the bus so why not?" He said, "You should read it when I'm done."

"Maybe I will." I said as I went and washed my bowl. "Although reading about the end of the world while we are kind of living it is a little weird don't you think?"

"Maybe or maybe it will give me survival ideas." Aaron laughed.

"What's so funny?" Micah asked as he came out to the living room.

"Not much besides Aaron reading a zombie apocalypse novel." I answered. Micah just looked at me for a minute.

"Really? Can't you just look outside for that?" He asked, looking at him.

"Could but this is research for how to survive." Aaron answered.

"Right I'm grabbing food." Micah said and headed for the kitchen, shaking his head.

Aaron went back to reading and I watched the smoke out the window. Not long after everyone was up and there was constant chatter as background noise. It was a good reminder that we were all alive. I stopped watching the smoke to take in the people around me in their various activities.

"Quite the family we have, isn't it?" Aaron asked as he looked at me over the top of his book.

"Yeah seems so." I responded.

"Hey you seem kind of down. What's up?" he asked me, sitting up.

"Not down just been thinking, or I guess worrying would be a better word." I answered.

"About?" he asked.

"It seems like this trip is taking a long time and I worry we won't make it." I told him as he took my hand.

"Ash it's taking a long time because Sam and Tone are trying their best not to draw attention to us. They're staying away from where they think there might be a lot of people." Aaron said.

"Why are they avoiding people? Shouldn't we be trying to help as many as we can?" I asked, thinking of all the people we may have left to horrible ends.

"Don't want to chance running into the wrong sort." Aaron said.

"Wrong sort?" I asked.

"People like my brother, they would try and take the bus from us and where would we be without the safety of our home?" Aaron asked me. He was right, not everyone was out to help others. There were people out there that would only be out for themselves. Some people just won't care that the world was turned upside down. All they cared about is themselves, not who they hurt to insure they get safety or supplies.

"That why we've barely stopped?" I asked.

"Yeah, Sam doesn't like the area we're in right now. We were followed for a while yesterday before we stopped for gas. They gave up when we didn't stop but we could run into others who won't. So Sam is avoiding roads that have signs of frequent use." Aaron answered.

"Were we really being followed or could it have been someone just traveling the same way?" I asked.

"I don't know. Could have been either but we can't take chances that could cost us the thing that is really keeping us safe." Aaron said, "I know how my brother thought so at least I can give Sam some advice to help us."

"Your brother was a really bad guy, wasn't he?" I asked him and he put the book down.

"Yeah he was." He answered.

149

"So how did you turn out to not be like him?" I asked.

"I saw how he was to people and how people treated him for it. I didn't want to be like that. Though I did whatever he said to avoid his anger. I liked having people wanting to be my friends for me. Not because they were scared what would happen if they weren't." he answered, "Plus I had Emily."

"I'm sorry you grew up like that." I told him.

"Don't be. I have some skills that could be useful now. Besides there's no reason to regret the past that you can't change when there's a future ahead." He said and laughed, "Don't feel sorry for me."

It was hard to be upset around Aaron; he took what was thrown at him, dealt with it and moved on. Like now his past growing up sounded horrible but he was smiling, like it was nothing. I admired him and hoped his attitude would be one I could learn to get through the challenges we were bound to face.

Chapter Fourteen

I looked out the window to see a black lifted truck was riding up beside us. A guy in the passenger seat, his face obscured by his red beard and aviator style sunglasses was waving his arms trying to get Sam to roll down his window.

"What do you think Tone?" Sam asked.

"I don't see weapons yet. Window down and we don't have to pull over to see what they want." Tone answered as he shrugged. Sam nodded and hit the button to roll his window down.

"Howdy friend." Sunglasses called.

"Howdy." Sam called back.

"How bout y'all pull on over and we have a chat?" Sunglasses asked.

"No offense but we don't know you." Sam told him. "We aren't pulling over."

"Now come on, is that anyway to be?" Sunglasses asked.

"I'm sure you can understand we have kids to protect. We don't know you so we aren't pulling over." Sam told him and reached for the window button.

"Look friend I told you to pull the damn bus over." Sunglasses growled, "Either you pull it over or we shoot it over." Sam rolled the window up and nodded to Tone. Sunglasses started waving a gun where we could see it.

"Everybody get down!" Sam shouted as bullets started hitting the side of the bus. Sydney threw a gun to Aaron as Tone got a couple of spots set up for them to open windows to return fire.

Sam kept us moving at a steady pace, he didn't try to speed up. The guys in the truck could outrun us. We all heard when one of the back dual tires got hit. The bus swerved violently tossing us all to the side. The back end of the bus slammed into the truck sending it off the road where it rolled into the huge rainwater ditch on the side of the road.

"Is everyone okay?" Sam asked.

"Just a few bruises." Sydney told him as she went around and checked everyone.

"Anyone still following?" Sam asked.

"Not right now, can't even tell if anyone climbed out of the truck." Tone answered. Sam waited until he couldn't see the people who tried to ambush us. As soon as he felt we were safe he stopped and Tone went to check the damage done to the tire.

"The other one is fine but there's no way we can change the busted one." Tone was saying, "The bus is way too heavy for us to do it."

"Didn't we see something about there being a garage around here?" Sam asked, "Maybe we can figure it out there or find someone willing to take payment to help us."

"Yeah, I think I know which one you're talking about." Tone said, "That Jeb's Garage we saw the sign for. I can find it on the map and have us there in no time."

"Are we going to be safe at a garage?" I asked. My hands were shaking.

"I don't know. Could be that we get there and no one is there." Tone told me, "We're okay now. Sydney, Sam and I have been through worse than this."

Feeling the bus moving again even though it was slow going was more calming than staying in the middle of the road. Sam kept his eyes scanning the road making sure he was driving carefully. Sydney stayed in the living room with us splitting her attention between watching out the windows for more trouble and checking on all of us.

Tone's ability to figure out the map he had got us to the garage. There was a tall guy with dark hair standing with two boys. One had brown hair and the other was a blonde. They were outside working on boarding up windows to the house. They all stopped and turned when they heard the bus. When we pulled up, the oldest of the three waved at us and came over to Sam's window.

"Well how are y'all doing?" the guy asked, "I'm Jeb and these here are my boys, Jacob and Jesse."

"We need a new tire, ran into some trouble on the road a ways back." Sam answered. "Would you be able to help us get her all fixed up?"

"You didn't lead that trouble to my door did ya?" Jeb asked.

"No sir, we left it in a ditch." Sam answered. Jeb nodded.

"We can probably fix it up, but it won't be free." Jeb said.

"Am I right to think that money means very little anymore?" Sam asked.

"It don't do much right now." Jeb agreed.

"We have food and medical supplies." Sam offered.

"That would be an acceptable payment seeing how I do have family here to take care of." Jeb agreed. "Go ahead and back her into the garage. You and yours can go hang out in the house while my boys and I get her up and running again."

"Sounds good, it will sure be nice to sit in a house for a bit." Tone called back to Jeb.

Sam went ahead and got the bus all backed into the garage. We followed him into the old farm house. There was lemonade laid out on the table with cups, so Tone poured everyone a glass and we sat to wait. I was beginning to feel on edge about being off the bus and in a stranger's house.

"Sam, I'm going to go find a bathroom." I told him as I stood and made my way to the nearest hallway.

The first door I opened was not a bathroom. It reeked like an outhouse and there was a blonde woman chained to the wall by a collar around her neck. It looked padlocked. She turned when the door opened and I could see bald spots from where she had pulled her hair out. She had ice blue eyes and was foaming at the mouth; there were claw marks on her face and neck.

Her clothes were torn and there were more claw marks on the wall where the chain was securely bolted. She was watching me while moving her head side to side before she growled and ran at me. The chain stopped her but the force threw her onto her back as her legs came out from under her. I quickly backtracked out of the room and closed the door.

I tried the next door but this room was much the same only there was an old man sitting in a chair. He didn't have much hair left but he also didn't look like he had clawed himself up at all. The room had the same smell as the first one, but the guy in the chair didn't respond much to my being there.

He was watching me but not the way the woman had been. He started to growl slightly and I left him, shutting the door between us.

I tried one more door. It was the last one in this hallway. There was a blonde girl, who looked close to my age, in this one. The room smelled cleaner. She turned around to look at me and a look of surprise filled her ice blue eyes, the same eyes the woman in the first room had.

She had some claw marks near her neck, like she had tried to pry the collar off.

"Don't leave." She said when I turned to leave the room.

"Who are you?" I asked her, "Why are you chained up?"

"I'm Hannah, I'm Jeb's daughter." She answered.

"Why are you chained up?" I repeated.

"Three days ago when I was trying to feed Mama and Grandpa Archie, Mama bit me." Hannah explained, "Daddy is afraid I'll turn dangerous and take off like Mama did."

"You were bit?" I asked taking a step back.

"Wait! Don't leave! I've been in here three days." Hannah said as she took a step forward, the chain stopped her. "I haven't shown any symptoms like Mama and grandpa Archie did."

"If you're not showing symptoms why are you in here?" I asked.

"Daddy won't let me out; it took Mama and grandpa Archie less than two days to start showing symptoms." Hannah explained, her eyes kept darting back to the door.

"Why does he keep you all chained if he thinks you're dangerous?" I asked her.

"He thinks we'll get better so long as he feeds us and makes us take whatever medicines he gets his hands on." Hannah answered.

"Do you think he's right?" I asked.

"I've seen those monsters, that's what bit Mama. I don't want to be that. If there's really no hope for me I want someone to end this not only for me but for mom and grandpa Archie." She answered.

"I don't know if I can help with that. Your dad and brothers are fixing our tire and I don't think they wanted us to even see you guys, let alone kill you." I told her.

"I really haven't shown any symptoms; maybe you can get me out of here? Take me with you? You'll do what should be done if I do start showing anything right?" She asked and she sounded desperate. "Please, I know dad loves us and that's why he's doing this but it's cruel."

"Let me go talk to the guy who's kind of in charge of my group." I answered as I backed out the door.

"Just hurry, I can sneak into your vehicle without my dad or my brothers seeing me." She pleaded as I shut the door to go to Sam about what I had seen in the rooms and what Hannah had told me.

Sam took one look at my face and he got up to see what was wrong.

"Ashlyn?" Sam asked.

"Sam, Jeb has his daughter locked in a room and chained to a wall." I told him, "Her mom and grandfather are in other rooms and they're crazed. She got bit three days ago and hasn't shown any symptom. She wants us to get her out and to go with us."

"How long did her mom and grandfather take to show symptoms?" he whispered back.

"Less than two days from what she said." I told him.

"She knows if she goes with us and starts that we have no choice but to kill her before she can hurt us?" He asked.

"Yeah she said that's what she wants; she doesn't want to be a monster." I told him, "But the collar on her neck looks metal and there's a padlock on it. Can we get her out?"

"Last room down the hall?" he asked and I nodded. "I can see if I can pick the lock than if she can make it onto the bus without her family knowing we'll take her. Go sit with everyone else and don't say anything about this till we are on the bus and away from here."

I did as Sam told me to and went to sit next to Aaron. He looked at me before he leaned over.

"I heard what you two were saying. You're a good person Ash." He whispered and said nothing else.

159

I was on the edge of my seat waiting for Sam to come back. He returned just as the other door opened with Jeb walking in, followed by his sons. Jeb saw where Sam had come from and I could see the blonde boy looked mad.

"What were you doing back there?" Jeb asked.

"You know they'll turn and when they do they won't be them anymore. You'll be putting your boys at risk." Sam said instead of answering.

"No, you see my wife and dad got bit when they ran to the store. My daughter, Hannah got bit a few days ago but I can fix them, all they need is medicine and they'll get better." Jeb said explaining to Sam. "I had to chain them up, they aren't well and they aren't thinking. That's how Hannah got bit."

"He didn't have any right to go back there." the younger son, Jesse, screamed as he hurled a glass of lemonade he'd picked up.

It hit an old shelf that had a canister and a burning oil lamp on it. The shelf broke on impact sending its contents to the floor. The canister apparently had oil in it. Once the gas around the flame of the oil lamp broke the oil ignited into flames.

"Boys go get your mother, grandfather, and sister, now." Jeb screamed at the boys and they ran into the hallway. Before they emerged from the first room the fire consumed the mouth of the hallway. Leaving no way for them to come back out that way. The boys saw this and ran back into the first room.

Sam got everyone moving, running out of the burning house and towards the bus. Jeb was still standing waiting for his family, he wouldn't leave without them. Outside we saw that the window to that first room was boarded up from outside.

The boys wouldn't be able to get out that way. Sam made it to the bus first and got it started as the rest of us piled on. Hannah was sitting at the dining room table though nobody said anything to her yet.

"Everyone on?" Sam called out and Tone looked over us all doing a head count, his eyes stopped and stayed on Hannah.

"We've got everybody. Get us out of here." Tone responded. "You the daughter?"

"Yeah." Hannah answered.

"You go crazed I will shoot you." Tone told her and Sydney shot daggers at him with her eyes.

"You'd better." Hannah told him and looked out the window. The house was collapsing and the fire continued on to the garage as Sam made it to the end of the driveway.

Sydney was seeing to the cuts on Hannah's neck from the collar. We heard honking outside. Looking out of the window we saw there was a guy in an old pick-up truck flagging Sam down. Sam stopped and rolled his window down.

"Where's that fire at?" the guy asked, sounding panicked.

"The garage. Son, you don't want to go that way." Sam told him.

"Did they get out?" The guy asked.

"No son, they didn't make it." Sam told him.

"What happened?" The guy asked as his face paled.

"Jeb's youngest threw a glass and hit a shelf holding a lamp and oil. The whole house went up. It happened too fast." Tone told him.

"That was my family." The guy said.

"Look there's nothing for you that way, why don't you join us?" Sam told him.

The guy agreed and Aaron helped him unload the supplies he had been bringing back home with him on to the bus. He came on looking shell-shocked and gripping a lucky rabbit's foot in one hand. He had brown hair and ice blue eyes that were taking in all the faces on the bus. They landed on Hannah and he did a double take.

"You said they didn't get out." He said.

"They didn't, she was already on the bus when the fire started." Sam told him.

"You freed her?" he asked.

"Yes we did." Sam said and the guy walked over to Hannah and hugged her, lifting her off her feet.

"Well how bout we all do introductions?" Tone said, "I'm Antonio Varqez. Call me Tone"

"I'm Hannah Collins and this is my brother Hunter Collins." Hannah said.

"Sam Simon." Sam added.

"Micah Hender and she's Sawyer Raide." Micah said pointing to himself and Sawyer.

"I'm Ashlyn Glass and these two are Axel Bishop and Aaron Pierce." I told him including Axel and Aaron.

"Sydney Tyme." Sydney just waved.

"I'm Daisy Duke." Daisy said last.

"Wait like Dukes of Hazzard's Daisy Duke?" Hunter asked, "Seriously?"

"Yeah my mom was a fan. My brother's name is Luke Duke." Daisy responded, "My nana always said mom fell for my dad for his last name."

"Did you have a car named General Lee?" Hunter asked.

"Sam, did you have to pick up the backwoods garage boy?" Daisy asked as she gave Hunter a dirty look.

"Don't mind Daisy, she's a rock star and they can be moody." Tone laughed.

"No problem." Hunter said, "But Daisy, what kind of hair color is green?"

"What kind of name is Hunter?" she shot back as she went to her room and slammed the door behind her.

"Oh yeah, they're getting along great." Tone said to Sam. Sydney shot them a look that screamed 'shut up'. It was good to have some new faces with us again. I was glad we could get Hannah out of that house and it seemed that she and her brother were close. He cheered up when he saw her, I was thinking he may be sad about his family but he was worried more about his sister.

Chapter Fifteen

Daisy was pacing in her room when I went to check on her. She was staring at her feet as she took each step. I noticed she was holding on to a see through blue glass shoe. She glanced up when I closed the door behind me. I sat on her bed and watched her take three steps before turning around to take three more. She sighed before she finally sat down.

"Did Sam really have to pick him up?" she asked me as she fiddled with the shoe.

"Hunter?" I asked her, wondering why he had her so riled up.

"Yes Hunter." She practically growled, "Not only is he frustrating and annoying he had to be cute on top of that. Why are you smiling?"

"I didn't realize I was." I said as I put my hand over my mouth.

"You're laughing at me, aren't you?" She asked, watching me.

"Maybe a little but mostly cause I don't get why he's getting to you." I told her and she put her head on my shoulder.

"Well the only guys we have to choose from at this moment are three adults. One of which is gay. The other two are just a bit older than I like. Micah is with Sawyer. Axel is a bit young," She said, "Then we pick up Hunter and I don't know, he's good looking and he's picking on me."

"Well maybe he's picking on you because he doesn't know what to do about you. Maybe he thinks you're good looking too." I told her. She looked like she was going to say something but changed her mind; she was smiling now, though.

We were both thrown on to the bed as the bus jolted and shook.

"Sorry for the rocky ride guys. If I would have stopped, they would have swarmed us so everyone hold on and try to keep each other from getting hurt." Sam said as we started going faster and there were even more bumps.

I forced myself up and out to the main living area.

"What happened?" I asked as Aaron kept me from flying into Hunter's lap.

"Red Eyes. A whole horde of them started coming at the bus. All we could do was try to go through them but we are running a lot of them over." Aaron told me as he grabbed Hannah before she hit her head on the table.

"Whoa hey now." Hunter said to Daisy as a particularly rough bump sent her into the air.

He pulled her down on to his lap and had his arms around her like a seat belt.

"Thanks." She said to him and stayed where she was.

"Do you think the fire is attracting them?" Sawyer asked as Micah kept her from bouncing around by keeping his legs over hers.

"Maybe, all I know is that there is a bunch of them." Tone answered, "Sam do we have a plan if we can't get through?"

"The plan is to get through." Sam answered.

Everyone got quiet and was holding on to each other. With every bump there was more banging noises around the bus.

"Don't worry we are also on a dirt road so not every bump is a Red Eye." Aaron told me as if he had read my mind.

"What?" I asked him.

"Sorry was thinking out loud." He responded as the bumps were becoming fewer and farther between each one.

167

"We're through." Sam said and everyone cheered, Daisy kissed Hunter. She pulled away and he looked like he was lost in her eyes before she got up and went to her room. She winked at me as she walked by.

"Whoa." Was all Hunter managed to say. Micah looked between him and Daisy's closed door and started laughing. Hunter looked at him and I noticed he was blushing a bit, guess he did think Daisy was good looking after all.

It started to storm outside. A few fat raindrops hitting the windshield hard as the wind kicked up rocking the whole bus. Sam kept driving, determined to get us to someplace safer than this. Tone was watching out the window, as it felt like the bus tilted off the ground on one side.

"Sam we have to find shelter to park in or this wind will tip the bus." Tone told him as he held the dash for dear life.

"Where Tone? Do you see any place?" Sam yelled at him.

"There's a hotel up ahead." Tone told him, "Could just drive straight into the lobby, park as close to the back as we can. Looks like one has a glass wall to show off how nice it is."

"What if there are people in there?" Sam asked, reluctant to stop.

"Well without the bus we're up shit creek with no damn paddle." Tone told him.

"Tone's right Sam, we have to take the chance of dealing with people. We can't stay in this storm it's only going to get worse." Sydney said as she held on to the dining room table.

Sam didn't argue he just changed the direction the bus was going and aimed for the huge glass windows. We crashed through and could see pieces of glittery glass raining down all around us. Sam kept going till he got to an area big enough to turn the bus around.

"Anyone hurt?" Sam said.

"Think everyone is good." Sydney answered.

"We may have another problem." Aaron said.

I looked over to where he was standing. He was holding one of the open cabinet doors.

"What?" Tone asked.

"We've been cleared out." Aaron answered.

"What do you mean?" Sydney asked.

"Food is gone." Aaron responded.

Sam and Tone joined Aaron in the kitchen.

"That bastard." Tone said.

"What?" Sydney asked.

"Jeb. Him and his sons were alone with the bus." Tone answered.

"Shit. Search the bus and take inventory of what else is missing." Sam directed.

Sawyer and I went to check our room.

Nothing looked out of place at first. Sawyer discovered that our panties were missing.

Disturbed we headed back to see what Sam wanted us to do now.

"Inventory?" Sam asked once everyone was gathered together again.

"They hit our medical supplies hard, we're down to three first aid kits." Tone answered.

"They didn't find the ammo but they did take the guns we weren't carrying." Sydney said.

"The pervs took my panties." Daisy said.

"Ours too." Sawyer added. The thought felt a lot like spiders running over my body.

"Gross." Axel said.

"This is bull shit." Aaron said, his fists clenching at his sides.

"Yes, it is but we're here now and from the looks of it no one else is here." Sam said, "So what do we do now?"

"Search the hotel for food." Aaron suggested, "Send people out to hunt."

"How would we hunt; all we have are a couple hand guns?" Sydney asked.

"There has to be a sporting goods store somewhere, maybe we'll find something there." Aaron said.

"You all heard him, let's see what we can find here." Sam said and led the way off the bus.

"How do they have light here?" Sawyer asked and I realized she was right, there shouldn't be any light.

"Generators probably, kicked on whenever the power went." Sydney answered.

"If there was light why isn't anyone here?" Daisy asked.

"Lights might scare people now. Not knowing who controls them. They're better avoided." Sam answered.

"Break into pairs and see what you can find." Tone said, "Axel and Sydney, you okay to stay with the bus?"

"You got it." Sydney answered.

"Ash you're with me." Aaron said, "We're heading upstairs."

Chapter Sixteen

I was looking up the thirteen stories worth of stairs contained in the stairwell.

"Why can't we take the elevator?" I asked.

"Don't trust the generator and may miss someone hiding." Aaron answered.

He started up the stairs. I watched him go up the first five steps before I groaned and followed him.

"I hate stairs." I said.

"Hate them as you climb." Aaron said.

I groaned.

One hundred and fifty something steps later we were standing in the deserted hallway of the thirteenth floor. It was labeled fourteenth floor due to some superstition, as the number thirteen was deemed bad luck.

Aaron was a staying only a few steps ahead of me. He was tense as he stopped at the first door and knocked. After listening for a minute, he stepped back and kicked the door in.

The room was empty.

"Little dramatic don't you think?" I asked.

"How?" Aaron responded as he opened the bathroom door.

"Kicking in the door. What was with the knocking anyway?" I asked.

"Seeing if anyone was in here." He answered.

"Like someone would open the door for you?" I responded.

"No." He said, "More a check for Red Eyes."

"Ah, they would have reacted to the knocking." I said.

"There's nothing useful in here.' Aaron said.

I followed him out of the room and to the next door.

Aaron knocked.

A loud thump shook the door causing me to scream and jump away.

"That's why I knock." Aaron said.

"I said I got that." I told him.

"Just checking."

"How do we do this?" I asked.

"I kick in the door; you stab the dead thing." Aaron said.

"Okay." I said, "Do you have something for me to stab with?"

"Yeah." He said and handed over his blade from its sheath on his belt.

The wood handle fit my hand well. The blade had 'Winchester Limited Edition 2006' inscribed on it. The tip of the blade was chipped.

"Ready?" Aaron asked.

I nodded and took a deep breath as he kicked the door in.

The door swung in slamming into the Red Eye's face knocking him to the floor.

I threw myself on top of him and aimed to bring the blade down into his eye.

As I brought the blade down, I noticed his green eyes.

I was already screaming as the blade slid into his left green eye.

The man was limp when the hilt was stopped by his socket.

I couldn't stop screaming.

"Ashlyn look at me." Aaron said.

His hands were on my shoulders as he shook me. His blue-green eyes came into focus. His lips were moving but I couldn't hear him.

His lips kept moving.

"I killed him." I said.

"Ashlyn, stop." Aaron said.

"I killed him." I was stuck on repeat.

"Look at his arms." Aaron said as he shook me again, "Ashlyn, look at his arms."

I looked away from Aaron and to the man's arms.

There were bites. Red and raw.

"He was already dead." Aaron said.

"His eyes—"

"Don't think that." Aaron said.

He pulled me away and forced me to look at him.

"You know what bites mean." He told me.

I nodded and let Aaron lead me out of the room.

I noticed the door number fourteen-thirteen.

Whoever designed the hotel missed a thirteen.

I started laughing while I was crying.

I put my back against a wall and slid down to the ground till I could wrap my arms around my knees. Aaron squatted down in front of me.

"Breathe." He said.

"I can't."

"Yes you can. We still have work to do." Aaron told me, "Focus on that."

I wiped my eyes. The laughing caused hiccups.

I forced myself to stand up as I held my breath and counted to thirty.

Aaron waited until I got the hiccups to stop before leading to next door.

He knocked.

There was nothing from inside. He continued on.

"Are we not going in?" I asked.

"Maybe on the way back." He answered, "You need time to calm down and I want to see what I can see from the windows up here."

The closer we got to the window at the end of the hallway, the more blood was becoming visible. The window was broken, but there was no glass on the floor. The wind from the storm was whipping the tattered curtains in at us.

"Something went out." Aaron said.

"Looks like." I agreed.

The cool storm air helped clear my head. I could see green eyes but I could also see bites.

"How are you holding up?" Aaron asked.

I shrugged and looked out the broken glass, anywhere to avoid looking at Aaron's eyes.

"Ash you'll be fine." Aaron said, "You have me."

"I know I just keep seeing green eyes." I said.

"I know, and I keep seeing bites." He responded.

"What did you want to see from up here?" I asked.

"Was hoping to see if I can see shops around, this storm isn't going to let me." Aaron answered.

"Sporting goods store?" I asked.

"That was the hope." He said.

"Now what?" I asked, "Are we going to go regroup?"

"Yeah I want to see who can hunt." Aaron answered.

"I've never hunted." I said.

"I know." He said.

"Don't leave me." I said.

"You know I wouldn't." he reassured.

"Thank you."

"You'll still have to learn to hunt." He said.

He turned away from the window and started leading the way back to the stairwell.

Chapter Seventeen

Standing with Sam, Aaron recounted everything we saw upstairs.

"So they only person you found was someone who was bit?" Sam asked.

"Yeah we didn't search every room." Aaron said.

"That's understandable." Sam said.

"Storm is making visibility impossible." Aaron said.

"You mentioned hunting?" Sam asked.

"Going back up first thing to see what's around here." Aaron answered.

"I asked around and found four people who have hunting skills." Sam said.

"Who do we got?" Aaron asked.

"Hunter, Hannah, Daisy, and Tone." Sam answered.

"I think three groups of two." Aaron answered.

"I'll ask around again and find you a sixth." Sam responded.

"I got one." Aaron said, "Ash stays with me."

Sam nodded and went around to gather everyone up.

Aaron nodded to me and raised a water bottle. When I nodded he threw a bottle to me.

Hannah came over passing out an open can to everyone.

"I know it's not much, but it's what was in the kitchen." She said when she handed me a can of corn.

With no utensils I tilted the can up and drank the corn. It was better than nothing. I wasn't the only one drinking my dinner. Everyone had open random canned goods as they came to join Aaron and me near the bus.

Sam was the last to come back. He stood watching all of us.

"Aaron has a plan." Sam started.

"What would that be?" Sydney asked.

"A group of people have been picked to be hunters." Sam answered.

"How are we hunting?" Sydney asked, "It's not like we can take the bus to the woods."

"Yeah and who knows what's around here?" Sawyer said.

"Well—" Sam said.

"Naw I got this." Aaron interrupted.

Sam nodded his consent and stepped back.

"First we're not taking the bus. We will find vehicles and use them." Aaron said.

"And weapons?" Sydney asked.

"Going to see what we find." Aaron said.

"Who's the team?" Sydney asked.

"Hunter, Hannah, Daisy, Tone, Ashlyn, and Aaron." Sam answered.

"So get some sleep. There will be plans by morning." Tone said.

Even with the hotel around us, as soon as it was suggested to sleep everyone made their way back on to the bus. The close quarters felt safe. Aaron squeezed my hand as I walked by him.

"Ash, wake up." Aaron shook me awake.

Green eyes were still in my mind as I sat up.

"Storms done and sun's up. Let's go and have a look around" He said.

"Okay." I responded and followed him.

I groaned when we got to the stairwell. So many stairs.

Aaron started up, he stopped five steps up and looked down at me. He raised an eyebrow at me.

I groaned and started up the steps.

When we got to the door labeled fourteenth floor I froze.

"Ash, I wouldn't take you up here if I hadn't cleaned up first." Aaron told me as he pushed open the door.

"If you've already been up here, why are we here now?" I asked.

"I came back up with Tone last night." Aaron answered.

"So what are we doing?" I asked. All the doors in the hall were open now.

"We're here to see." Aaron said.

Now that there was the grey daylight from the predawn we could see the body that broke the window. It was lying speared on the balcony below. There was no way to tell if it was a man or a woman.

"Ash see the trucks over there?" Aaron asked. He was pointing at a filled parking lot not far from the hotel.

"Yeah." I answered.

"It looks like it's a dealership." He said.

"That solves the vehicle issue." I said, "Looks like there's a sign to the left, can you read it?"

Aaron looked where I was pointing and squinted his eyes.

"Reggie's Outdoor Sporting." He said, "Or at least I think it says that."

"If you read that right so you think there might be weapons there?" I asked.

"We can check when we take the others and walk over to that dealership." He answered.

"Walk?" I asked, "Wouldn't it be safer to take the bus?"

"Think it would be safer to walk." He answered, "We would be less noticeable."

"I guess six people blends better than a giant green bus." I said and kicked at the wall.

"We'll be fine Ash." Aaron said.

"Should we go get the others and let Sam know?" I asked.

"Let's do it." He said.

We headed back down the stairs and to the bus. Tone was stretching by the door as we walked up. He nodded to us.

"Able to see what's around this morning?" Tone asked.

"Yeah." Aaron answered.

"Looks like a car dealership close by and a maybe a sporting goods store." I added when Aaron stayed quiet.

"That sounds promising." Sam said from the doorway of the bus.

"Just need the others and want to head out." Aaron said.

"On foot?" Sam asked.

"Less noticeable." Aaron answered.

"Smart thinking." Sam responded, "I'll go wake the troops."

Tone had gone back on to the bus with Sam and returned with a box. He handed me a can of pineapples and one I couldn't read to Aaron.

"Breakfast." He said and sat down on a chair that had been dragged over.

Tone handed everyone who came out their own can. Once we were all gathered he sent a can opener around.

"Aaron and Ashlyn went up and have found a couple places for the hunting group to check out." Sam explained as we all drank our cans of fruit.

"Are we all going?" Sawyer asked.

"No they're going on foot." Sam answered, "They'll see what they find and return here."

"What if they don't come back?" Axel asked.

"We'll give them till afternoon and if they're not back we're continuing on to Paradis." Sam responded.

"Wait." Sawyer said, "You sound like if they're not back we'll leave them."

"That is what I'm saying." Sam answered.

"We can't just leave them." Sawyer said.

"I'm not going to just abandon them, but we have other people to think of too." Sam said.

"Plus we know where we're heading." Tone said.

"So if we don't make it back before Sam wants to move out, we'll find you on the road." Hunter added in.

"I guess." Sawyer said.

"Let's get a move on." Aaron cut in.

He had a backpack slung over his shoulder and two more sitting at his feet. Hunter grabbed one while Tone took the last one.

"What's in the bags?" Daisy asked.

"Couple bandages, pain relievers, ointments, can of soup, water bottles, and Ramon noodles." Aaron answered.

"Sounds like we're ready." Tone said.

"See you all soon." Sam said.

"See you on the other side, boss." Tone said.

Aaron led us out the front entrance of the hotel. There was a sign that looked like stained glass.

Petalite Springs Resort.

We had crashed into the highest ranked luxury resort in the state.

"Aaron." I said, "Do you see where we are?"

"Huh." He responded, "People said I'd never see this place."

"Weapons or vehicles first?" Tone asked.

"Vehicles." Aaron answered.

Chapter Eighteen

I was lagging behind the group. My calves were burning from the uphill slope. Aaron had the backpack with the water bottles. I forced myself to keep moving forward.

The ground leveled out and my legs felt like liquid as I caught up to the group. I sat down as soon as I was next to Aaron.

"It seems quiet." Tone said.

"Isn't that good?" Hannah asked.

"I don't know." Tone answered, "I was thinking we'd see people or at least Red Eyes."

"If there's people they may be hiding." Hunter said.

"And the Red Eyes?" Daisy asked.

"Keep an eye out and keep moving." Aaron said.

"The dealership is coming up how do you want to do this?" Tone asked.

"I worked at one and I know where they keep the keys." Hunter said.

"We pick off road vehicles and send Hunter for the keys." Aaron responded.

As we walked up you could see the spots where someone had come and took a vehicle. The glass to the office and showroom was shattered. Aaron led us straight to the trucks and SUVs.

"Pick your poison." He said.

"I'll take the green Wrangler." Tone responded.

"I want the black Dodge 3500." Aaron said.

"I'll take the Ranger." Hunter said.

"That orange thing?" Tone asked.

"Yeah." Hunter said, "I'm going for the keys."

"Want help?" Aaron asked.

"No I'll move quicker by myself." He answered.

Hunter walked between two big trucks and disappeared from where I could see him. Aaron jumped up into the bed of the nearest truck and watched the direction Hunter had gone in. I was starting to notice the quiet Tone had pointed out. We hadn't seen anything moving.

I wandered between a couple of SUVs to an empty spot. The breeze blew an old flyer to my feet.

'One weekend only sale.' It read across the top.

There was a yellow sneaker lying by a tire of a blue truck. I walked over to it.

As I got closer I could see the leg that was still attached.

I covered my mouth and forced myself not to scream. I stepped back and came up against someone.

I turned around ready to swing.

Aaron grabbed my wrist before I could hit him.

"Whoa." He said.

"Sorry." I told him.

"What freaked you out?" He asked.

"Just look." I answered and pointed to the yellow sneaker.

Aaron went and checked it out. He walked all the way around to the other side of the truck.

"Ash you need to see this." He called to me.

I forced myself to walk over to him.

There were rust splatters everywhere. Old blood. The leg was still attached to a whole body. Her throat was missing.

"Why did you want me to see?" I asked. I was gagging at the sickly-sweet decaying smell.

"This is the only thing we've seen." He said.

"Yeah." I responded.

"Where is everyone now?" He asked.

"I don't know if I want to find out." I said, "I just want Hunter to get back with the keys so we can leave."

"Ash really look at her." He said.

"Why?" I asked.

"Her only injury is her throat." He answered.

"I saw that." I said.

"If Red Eyes did this there would be more injuries." He pointed out.

"I didn't think about that." I said.

"Let's look around a bit more over here." He said.

I followed him between the vehicles. Now there was more blood. We were getting closer to an open garage. The parking lot was less packed over here. There were also people scattered throughout the cleared space. Dead people.

All of them were only missing pieces and appeared uninjured beyond what was gone. The man closest to us was missing both legs. Another man was missing his arms.

Something clattered to the ground in the garage. Aaron pulled me behind a white sedan. He had his finger to his mouth.

"What did you break now?" A man's voice asked.

"Nothing, I just bumped the table." Another man answered.

"Make sure you didn't wreck any of Roger's supplies." The first man said.

"Believe me I wouldn't risk that." The other responded, "I like to eat not be eaten."

"Have you seen Kendal since she went to patrol?" The first asked.

"Haven't seen her yet. She's probably with Taylor." The other answered, "You know how those girls are Mitch."

"Yeah Don, I know." Mitch responded, "They're lucky they have something Roger wants, otherwise they wouldn't be here now."

"We'd better get the meal started before Roger gets back." Don replied.

"How long did Roger say he'd be gone?" Mitch asked.

"He said he'd be back for dinner. He wants the blonde tonight." Don said.

I looked at Aaron. He shook his head and put his finger to his mouth.

"You going to help me get her?" Mitch asked.

"Fine." Don responded.

We heard a door close.

"Back to the others." Aaron whispered.

I nodded.

He kept hold of my hand as we made our way back to our group. Hunter was just coming back with the keys when we walked up.

"You two okay?" Hannah asked.

"No we got to move out now." Aaron said.

"What happened?" Tone asked.

"Cannibals." Aaron answered.

"Serious?" Hunter asked.

"Yes, let's move now." Aaron said holding his hand out for the keys to the black pick-up.

Hunter handed out the keys and the teams loaded into their chosen vehicles. Aaron pulled out first leading everyone away from the dealership and towards the sporting goods store. I kept checking behind us, waiting for someone to chase us.

I didn't even notice when we pulled up to the store.

Aaron turned off the truck and my heart pounded in my chest.

Hunter parked on our driver side while Tone pulled up to the passenger.

Even after everyone unloaded, no one said anything until we were sure no one was around and we were inside the walls of the store.

This place looked like I expected everything to look. Racks were knocked over, shelves were picked clean. The only items left appeared to be broken.

Aaron, Hunter, and Hannah spread out picking up things from the floor. Aaron was smiling with every discovery he made. I didn't understand why he was happy, he was holding pieces.

"I can't believe these got left." Aaron said.

"What do you got there?" Hunter asked.

"Bows." Aaron answered.

"What's wrong with them?" I asked.

"Nothing. They're just not strung." Aaron answered.

"Why would they be left if nothing's wrong?" I asked.

"Bunch of reasons." Hunter answered.

"Like what?" I asked.

"Someone didn't know how to string them or couldn't find the string." Hannah answered, "Or someone who thought a crossbow would be better."

"Doesn't really matter what they thought." Aaron said.

"Their leavings are our gain." Tone said.

"Do we have everything we need for them?" I asked.

"Sure do." Hunter answered.

Daisy was staying quiet over by a window.

"What's up?" Hannah asked her.

"Do you guys hear that?" She asked.

Everyone stood still and listened.

In the distance there was the rumble of an engine.

It was getting closer.

"I vote we load up and head back to the bus." Tone suggested.

"I second that." Hunter said.

We were on our way back to Petalite Springs Resort. Aaron made sure to lead away from the approaching engine. I still kept a look out for someone following us.

Aaron stopped the truck in front of the broken window we had driven through with the bus.

The bus was gone.

"What do we do?" I asked.

"It's still early they should have still been here." Aaron said.

"Something must have happened." Tone called from his open window.

"So we head to Paradis and hope we find them on the road." Aaron responded.

Tone took the lead as we headed back to the road with the hopes that we would see the bus on the way.

Trisha Leazier

Chapter Nineteen

It wasn't long before we came across a fence stretching across the road. Our bus was also stopped there. Tone pulled up to the passenger side. Hannah and him both grabbed everything out of the Wrangler and went back on to the bus.

Aaron pulled up to the driver side and waved to Sam.

"Glad to see you all found us." Sam called once he had his window down.

"Why'd you leave early?" Aaron asked.

"Had to. People showed up." Sam answered.

"People?" Aaron asked.

"Yeah a man. Called himself Roger." Sam answered, "Called the hotel his hunting ground."

"Everyone get out okay?" I asked.

"Yeah we got lucky and everyone was already on the bus." Sam responded.

"He didn't follow you?" I asked.

"That was the weird part." Sam said, "But now there's this fence."

The fence went well into the trees on either side and didn't look like there was a way we could get around it. Someone pulled up behind us blocking the way. Another truck drove up beside our truck.

"The way's blocked we'll have to turn around." Sam told the stranger who started laughing.

"Oh, we know it's blocked, it's our fence." The guy said as he watched Sam for a reaction.

"Well we'll be on our way then, if your friends would be so kind as to move out of our way." Sam explained as another guy walked up. This guy was obviously the leader, everyone backed away from him as he walked by.

"See, now there, we have a problem." The leader said as he took the other guys place by Sam's window.

"How do we have a problem?" Sam asked. I could see he was tense.

"We want your bus and you can't go forward with the fence there. You can't go backwards since we got you blocked." The leader said.

"Who the hell are you?" Sam asked. He gripped the steering wheel hard and his knuckles were losing color.

"They call me Captain and we're land pirates, you see our black flag flying there above our camp." Captain answered.

"Land pirates?" Sam responded.

"Yeah you come through our territory and we take what we want." Captain answered.

"We can give you some supplies to buy our passage." Sam told him.

"We don't need supplies." Captain said.

"What do you want?" Sam asked.

"We want your fancy bus." Captain answered.

"Look we're trying to be reasonable. You're not taking this bus from us, I don't care who you are." Sam told Captain.

"Oh but you should, you see I got bit and look at me. I'm the picture of health. They can probably use my blood as a cure, but I won't let them without charging." Captain laughed as he spit foam from his mouth.

"Hate to break it to you but you don't look like a picture of health with that foam." Sam said.

"That foam doesn't mean anything." Captain argued

"Get the hell out of our way or we will start shooting." Sam responded

I saw Sydney moved into position by one of the windows where the pirates didn't see her.

"You ain't going nowhere with our bus and whatever is on it." Captain said as his people cheered and he made rude gestures at Sam. I saw Sam tap his finger a couple times before he nodded. Sydney fired off two shots quickly that put down a couple of Captain's men.

Captain's people pulled out their weapons. I dropped down below the windows as Sam hit the gas and went through the fence. Aaron waited till the bus was clear of the fence and hit the gas pulling us in line behind Hunter's orange Ranger.

The pirates all scattered screaming at Sam as they tried to stop the bus by climbing onto it. There were Red Eyes on the other side of the fence. They flowed into the hole and went after the pirates running instead of us.

One guy got a good grip on the bus and Sydney leaned out a window. She shot him in the leg. He let go and was swarmed by the Red Eyes. Sydney waited till his head was visible again. She fired off a shot straight into his forehead cutting him off mid scream.

We could hear screaming and gunfire outside. It grew fainter as Sam led us away putting distance between us and the pirates.

Sam pulled over when we were miles away from the pirates. I helped Aaron grab the supplies we had in our truck. Back inside the bus Hannah was on the couch bleeding.

"What happened?" Hunter asked as he noticed his sister.

"Return fire came through that window before she got down. I can't get the bullet; it seems to be wedged into the bone." Sydney told him.

"Can't you just leave it there and stop the bleeding?" Hunter asked as he lifted Hannah's head into his lap.

"I don't know. If I do she may lose the ability to use that arm and it could make it worse." Sydney was telling him as Aaron came over to where I was.

"You okay?" He asked me as he sat down beside me.

"Yeah. Is Hannah going to be okay?" I responded.

"I don't know." Aaron told me as he looked at Hannah, "Depends on when we can get that bullet out of her."

"So we have to get to Paradis Roulette before we can really help her." I stated as we watched Hannah cry. Hunter had taken off the hoodie he had been wearing and I saw the bite marks on his forearm. I stared for a minute before I realized that they were human.

"Hunter what are those marks?" I asked, "Were you bit?"

"Oh." He responded and looked at his arm, "Yeah, I got bit when Mama and grandpa Archie did. I was helping them escape when it happened I hid it from dad when I saw what he was going to do with them."

"So just like Hannah. No symptoms?" Sam asked, joining the conversation.

"None." Hunter answered.

"You should have told us." Sam said.

"Sorry sir, with everything going on I forgot." Hunter answered. Sam nodded.

"We have to get her arm wrapped and steady till we can get her someplace for help." Sydney said bringing all attention back to Hannah. I was impressed she wasn't screaming. Although looking at Hunter and seeing the expression on his face, I was thinking maybe it was more surprising that he wasn't screaming.

Sydney got Hunter to carry Hannah to the room she had been using. She would have a bed to lay on while we continued to head to Paradis Roulette. Tone found some pain killers to give her and a sedative so she could hopefully sleep till we had help for her.

Daisy brought a few extra pillows from her room to help make Hannah as comfortable as she could be in her state. Hunter looked haunted as he came back to the living room and sat on the recliner.

"We are going to keep her sedated for the rest of this trip." Sydney said, "I'll stay in the room with her but I want all of you to stay out so we can keep her still."

Hunter didn't look happy about not being able to be the one staying with his sister. He also didn't challenge Sydney. Daisy went and sat next to him and he let her hold his hand. I was watching them as Aaron came over and put a hand on my shoulder. He didn't say anything, just patted my shoulder and walked into the kitchen. Sawyer and Micah were starting a game of Life with Axel, which was good, it would get his mind off Hannah. I ended up following Aaron.

"It's quiet." He told me.

"Everyone's processing what happened. I think they all want to be respectful to Hunter." I responded catching a water bottle he threw to me.

"True I feel bad for Sam driving. He must be feeling the pressure to get to Paradis now." Aaron was saying as I took a drink of the water.

"I would not want to be in his shoes right now. He doesn't have it easy being the leader and all." I agreed.

"Come look at this." Sam called.

I followed Aaron to stand in the doorway of the front of the bus.

"What's up?" Aaron asked.

"You see that in the distance?" Sam asked, pointing to what looked like the sun reflecting off a giant mirror.

"Yeah I think." I answered.

"That's Paradis Roulette, we are close enough to see it right now, and we just have to get there." Sam said and Aaron patted him on the back as I looked at our destination.

It looked far away to me with a lot of things between us and safety. I could see Sam was determined to get us there.

"Are we going to make it?" I asked Sam, still looking out the window.

"We'll make it; just have to keep it together."
He answered.

"Are we going to have to hunt?" I asked

"I don't know, depends where we stop and how long this leg takes us." Sam answered.

"Aaron said we found cannibals at the dealership." I told him.

"That's what Tone had told me. I think Captain was part of that same group." Sam said.

"Do you think we'll run into more people like the pirates?" I asked.

"I hope not." Sam answered.

I went back to my room where I could just stare out the window. I could still see the building Sam had pointed out but it didn't look like it was getting any closer yet.

The sky outside was an angry grey color that blocked out sunlight. It made it look more like night than day outside. Sawyer came and sat with me. She watched out the window with me. She leaned her head against my shoulder.

"I missed you." She said.

"I missed you too." I responded.

"I was afraid I wouldn't see you again when Sam left the hotel." She said.

I wrapped my arm over her shoulders.

Outside there was movement in the trees. We could see they were human but they moved more like animals.

"Are they following us?" Sawyer asked after we had watched them for a while.

"Maybe or there's something out there and we just happen to be going in the same direction." I told her as one of them broke away from the group and charged the bus.

There was a sickening thud as it hit and bounced off. Others started doing the same thing, so soon we were hearing *thud, thud, thud* as one after another hit the side.

"What are they doing?" Sawyer asked, watching as another one charged.

"I think they're trying to stop us." I told her and pointed to where there were a couple of SUV's on their sides.

"They're hunting us using a technique that worked on other people passing by." Sawyer said as the group gave hitting us a couple more tries. The bus was too heavy for them to knock over the way they had the SUV's. They gave up and backtracked to wait for another vehicle. It was weird to think they may be finding ways to hunt.

"Do you think they might all be forming packs?" I asked and Sawyer looked back out the window.

"I don't know maybe they just find it's easier to get food all together." Sawyer answered.

Up ahead outside I saw that there was a car on the side of the road. There weren't any Red Eyes by it but there was a man standing there. I went to the front of the bus to get a better look. As we got closer I could see the man was fairly tall with dark hair and was wearing black rimmed glasses.

"Sam you have to stop." I told him and he looked at the man.

"Why?" he asked, "It could be a trap."

"That looks like it might be Dr. Minnow, the doctor who did my sister's surgery." I told him and he slowed down and rolled down the window. The man walked over quickly.

"Are you Dr. Minnow?" Sam asked once he was close enough.

"Yes I am." Dr. Minnow answered looking like he was trying to place Sam.

"Are you alone?" Sam asked which seemed to confuse the doctor more.

"Yes I barely made it away from those creatures back there but I ran out of gas." Dr. Minnow responded.

"Okay, grab your stuff you're coming with us. Bring any medical supplies you have, we have a girl with a bullet lodged into a bone in her arm." Sam told him. Dr Minnow hurried back to his car and grabbed a few bags then rushed back to board the bus.

"How long were you stuck?" Sam asked him.

"I've been there about a day, hiding in the car. I saw you coming and thought I'd take the chance you would stop." He responded then his eyes landed on me, "I know you."

"My sister was Marie Forde; you were her doctor for her heart transplant." I told him, "I'm Ashlyn. Our friend in the back is hurt. Can you help her, Dr. Minnow?"

"Please, call me Scott, and of course, take me to her." Scott told me as he dropped all but one of his bags and followed me back to where Hannah was.

Chapter Twenty

Scott kept Sydney back in the room with him but he wanted everyone else out of his way. We all sat where we could in the living room, waiting to hear if he could help or not. It seemed to take forever before the door opened and he came out alone.

"I got the bullet out and we got the wound properly bandaged. The girl needs rest, so Sydney said she'll stay with her while she sleeps. She said to tell Hunter she'll get him when she wakes." Scott said. You could almost see the relief in the air. He smiled as he looked at all of us.

"Thank you for picking me up." Scott said to Sam.

"Don't thank me, I was going to drive by, it's Ashlyn you should thank—she recognized you." Sam responded as he kept his eyes on the road.

"Well then, thank you Ashlyn." He said to me and smiled.

"We needed a doctor." I told him and shrugged.

"So I guess I was just in the right place at the right time." Scott said.

"I guess so." I told him and went back to sit on my bed again.

It was good to know that Hannah wasn't going to be in pain from the bullet anymore. However, we still needed to get her to safety to heal. I wasn't sure how I felt about Dr. Minnow now being on the bus with us but at the same time maybe he knew what was happening.

I wanted to ask him, but I was afraid he was going to answer yes and tell me that it had been one of the risks. I didn't want to think that Marie had agreed to something. That she knew it could cause something like what we were facing now.

Sawyer found me again and joined me. I could feel her shooting looks at me like she was trying to read what was going on in my head. After a while she stopped and watched out the window. We passed more vehicles that had found themselves on the side of the road. At least these ones weren't knocked over.

She looked like she was watching places that could be hiding Red Eyes more than anything else. There was a patch of blue sky showing through the clouds now like someone had punched a hole into the grey.

"How many people do you think the Red Eyes got back there?" Sawyer finally asked me.

"I don't know. I don't want to think about it." I told her as I looked at her.

"If Hannah wasn't hurt would you have had Sam stop to pick up Dr. Minnow?" She asked, not meeting my eyes. I got what she was saying. She wanted to know if I blamed him for what had happened to Marie and if I would have left him to die as some sort of payback.

"I don't think I could have let Sam drive by him." I told her and I caught the little sigh she tried to hide. "Do you really think so little of me?"

"No, just with him being Marie's doctor and all we've been through. We've all changed and I just wanted to make sure that wasn't something that had changed about you." Sawyer said all in one breath, making it barely understandable.

"I don't know how I feel towards the guy but he was alone and we did need a doctor for Hannah. I'm not making friends with him or anything but yeah." I told her trying not to be mad that she had thought I could leave someone to die.

I didn't say anything else and eventually Micah came looking for Sawyer. She went to join whichever game Axel had picked now. I felt bad that I was glad she wasn't in the room with me anymore.

I started to cry thinking about Marie, wondering what she would do if she was here right now. I know she would have stopped for Dr. Minnow as well, even if she blamed him. Thinking about Marie made me think about my parents. Would I see them again? Had they made it someplace safe? I turned so I was facing the window as I let myself cry for everything that was lost.

I cried until it seemed like all my tears dried up. I decided it was time to join the group again, I went and washed my face and went to grab another taco. I sat with Aaron at the dining room table and he smiled at me.

"You doing okay?" he asked me.

"Yeah, just needed to cry." I told him and he nodded.

"So how do you know the good doctor?" Aaron asked me.

"He was Marie's doctor for her heart transplant. Marie was one of the human trials. She was one of the first to become one of the crazed and a Red Eye." I told him and watched as he sat back and took it in. His face became blank and cold.

"Do you think he may have known?" Aaron asked.

"I don't think so. I mean, I know Marie signed papers pertaining to her being in a trail program. I don't think anyone could have seen this happening." I answered him, "I just have issues seeing him, it makes me think of Marie." Aaron stood up and went into the living room, I followed him.

He went straight up to Scott.

"Scott, you worked with the people that this started with, so please tell us, what's going on." Aaron stated in front of everyone drawing all their attention.

"Yes, I worked for Clydework but I don't know what's happening. Nothing like this happened in the animal testing we did." Scott responded, "The animals all did really well."

"How is it that both Hannah and I have been bitten but neither one of us has had any symptoms?" Hunter asked from where he was seated with Daisy on the couch.

"I don't know why that would be, but could I do some testing on you two when she's healed? Maybe there's an abnormality in your blood and since you are related it's in both of you." Scott said.

He looked like his mind was already trying to solve the problem, like it was just an equation on a board.

"I'd have to talk to Hannah when she wakes up." Hunter said as he watched the doctor.

"Let me know, maybe the answers are in your blood." Scott repeated.

No one had anything to say to that and the conversation faded to silence. Some people from the group headed out of the room and to their rooms to be away from the tension that we were now drowning in.

Almost everyone had already headed to bed when Sam decided that we should stop for the night and rest. He pulled the bus off the road a bit to be out of the way, where people would leave it alone. Tone switched seats with Sam so if we had to leave quickly there would be fresh eyes on the road. I stayed in the living room with Aaron; I felt better knowing he was on the other couch. Scott went and slept on the floor in the room with Sydney and Hannah in case they needed him during the night.

The sun was barely turning the sky pink when I noticed the smell of meat cooking. I found Aaron and Hunter working in the kitchen together.

"Did you guys go hunt?" I asked as I rubbed sleep from my eyes.

"Yeah, only managed to get a few rabbits." Hunter answered.

"It's enough to feed everyone." Aaron said.

Tone started the bus to get us on our way. The bus rocked forward but didn't move.

"Sam we got a problem." Tone was telling Sam as Aaron headed to the door to check out what was going on. He came back looking grim.

"We got the back tires sunk in mud." He announced, "I'm going to take the old clothes out and see if we can get some traction to get us out of here."

"I'll come out with you." Sam told him and hauled himself out of his seat.

"Me too." I added and sat up. We were heading out the door when Micah, Hunter, Daisy, and Sawyer came out of their rooms. They followed us outside and saw what we were facing with the tires stuck into the mud.

"I'm going to get the clothes as much under those tires as I can." Aaron told them.

"How about after that, when Tone tries to move it again, we all try pushing and see if we can add some force to get it out." Hunter added and Aaron nodded. Once Aaron had the clothes set up as best he could he nodded to Sam.

"Tone let's give it a shot." Sam called out to Tone and he started pressing the gas as we all pushed. The bus didn't budge. Sam looked defeated.

"We need to get what we need off the bus and get to walking." He said to all of us as Tone leaned out the door of the bus to see what was going on.

"It's going to be hard to move Hannah." Hunter was saying.

"Hey before everyone starts panicking, let's give this one more shot." Aaron said making everyone look at him.

"Better be quick. Looks like we've got company." Tone said pointing to a group of Red Eyes heading our way. I counted at least fifteen of them but I kept losing count as they moved.

"Tone if we get the bus out don't stop until you get back onto the paved road. We'll catch up but if the bus gets stuck again we're done." Sam called into the door.

Aaron was throwing more of the clothes he had grabbed under the tires. He joined us at the back as soon as he was done and put himself in position next to me. Sam followed him over and found an open spot between Daisy and Sawyer to place himself.

"Go Tone!" He yelled and Tone hit the gas.

The bus lurched forward and we all pushed with everything we had. The bus kept going, spilling all of us onto the wet ground behind it. Looking up, I saw the Red Eyes were almost on us. Tone got the bus back onto the solidness of the paved road, then the first Red Eye made a grab for Daisy.

She screamed and kicked as Hunter grabbed her under her arms and pulled her away. He got her onto her feet and sent her running towards the bus before he turned and kicked the one off Micah.

Aaron had Sawyer on her feet and got her heading to the bus with Micah right on her heels. Next he turned to me while Hunter held off the Red Eyes that got too close. Sam was ahead of us heading to the bus.

Scott was standing outside the bus helping everyone get on. Hunter was right behind us as we ran, I heard him fall and turned grabbing Aaron as I stopped. We got Hunter back up between us.

The Red Eyes were catching up as we jumped onto the bus. Followed by Scott who was reaching for the door as the bus started moving. He stumbled forward missing the door. Sam caught him by his shirt and pulled him back kicking the door shut as he did. We all stayed on the floor panting as Micah started to laugh.

"You know we were almost Red Eye kibble, what's so funny?" Daisy demanded.

"We survived a scene straight out of a horror movie." Micah gasped between laughter.

"He's right." Aaron added agreeing and shaking his head.

"Yeah, if this was a movie what would they call it?" Tone called from the front of the bus.

"The wheels on the bus." Hunter answered as both Daisy and he gave into laughter. Even Sam was laughing as he joined Tone at the front of the bus.

"That was too close." Tone said as he glanced into the rearview mirror at us.

"Yeah, but Aaron was right to try again, which means we're not walking." Sam agreed.

Chapter Twenty-One

I didn't know how long we had been driving while we all recovered from the adrenaline that had run its course. The laughter had died down leaving silence. Sydney had come out and made sure everyone had eaten but she quickly returned to Hannah's side.

"Sam, I hate to tell you this, but we're going to need gas." Tone said, breaking the silence.

"Can we make it till it gets closer to dark so we can park near the station for the night?" Sam asked and Tone stayed quite while he thought.

"No, we have till about lunch then we'll have to stop." Tone answered.

"Okay." Sam said after a minute. "Next gas station you see we'll stop. By the time we eat we should be away from places people might hide to set up an ambush."

Tone nodded and kept watching the road. He tapped Sam when he saw one that looked clear. As we pulled up a man came out and waved to us. Sam looked like he'd rather keep driving but since Tone was driving, we stopped. Tone rolled down his window and the man came up to it.

"Hello there." The red-haired man greeted, "I'm Evan Smith, welcome to my station."

"Your station?" Tone asked.

"Yes sir. Got myself all set up inside and been getting food as payment for filling people up." Evan answered and smiled making his blue eyes look playful.

"How are you keeping the Red Eyes away?" Sam asked and Evan looked a little sheepish, the smile leaving his eyes.

"Red Eyes? That's what you call them? I've been calling them Shadows, but heard all sorts of names for them." Evan said, "I keep them out with a perimeter I set up. It's of cut up Shadows. Keeps them immobilized, but the others seem to stay away since they don't smell me over them."

"Gruesome, but smart." Tone responded.

"Yeah, I got them out of sight, don't want to scare people." Evan said.

"People will stop coming this way." Sam said, "Why don't you fill us up and come with us?"

"I'll be fine here; people won't stop coming." Evan said as he hooked up the pump to fill the bus up. Sam was watching him the whole time. "You are all set."

"Look, I'm serious about people not coming this way. The Red Eyes are figuring out how to stop people." Sam told him, "You should come with us, you have skills we could use and we have plenty of room."

"Where are you heading?" Evan asked, looking like he was thinking about the offer.

"Paradis Roulette, it's in a bio dome." Sam answered.

"Has the outbreak happened there?" Evan asked.

"No." Sam answered.

"What makes you so sure it won't happen?" Evan questioned.

"We're not, but our chances in there are better than our chances out here." Sam responded. "With what we've seen on the road we would be leaving you to die if we drive away without you."

"Why are you so sure people won't make it this way?" Evan asked.

"The Red Eyes are staying to the side of the road and charging cars. There's a bunch they've knocked over, we made it because we are in a heavy bus." Sam responded and Evan's eyes widened with the thought of Red Eyes having the capability to think.

It was scary that they were thinking enough to figure out how to get to people inside cars.

"Well you have convinced me that going with you is my best chance for survival." Evan finally said after thinking. "Let me go get my stuff."

"Sam do you know what you're doing?" Tone asked once Evan was out of earshot.

"He's been here for a while and he figured out how to keep the Red Eyes away. That's a skill we might need even after getting to my nephew." Sam responded.

"Why would we need a skill like that after we get to the dome?" Tone asked as he watched for Evan's return.

"As Evan said, we are not sure if the outbreak will stay at bay once we are in the dome. Plus if it does happen there we need to be able to survive." Sam responded as Evan came out walking with a bag slung over his shoulder and a wagon dragging behind him.

"What's in the wagon?" Tone asked as he jumped out to help Evan load up.

"The food I have. Figured I'd add it to what you have if we're all together now." Evan said as he handed over the bag to Hunter.

"Welcome aboard." Hunter greeted as Evan stepped onto the bus.

"Thank you." Evan responded and bowed his head slightly, "Now I assume you all know my name—who am I traveling with, may I ask?"

Hunter went around the bus and introduced Evan to everyone in turn. Evan shook everyone's hands and met their eyes as he was told their names.

"How did you figure out the Red Eyes wouldn't come around if they smelled others like them?" Axel wanted to know, speaking out what most of us were thinking.

"By accident actually. I was attacked and by the end was too tired to drag the bodies away I couldn't even make it to cover. I woke up and the other shadows just walked by me, the bodies had covered my scent and saved me." Evan explained.

"That was lucky for you." Aaron commented.

"Yes it was and I found that if I set up the perimeter with them they wouldn't come sniffing about." Evan said.

"Why do you call them shadows?" Sawyer asked.

"Because they are shadows of the people they once were." Evan answered, "Not really any different then you calling them Red Eyes."

Evan went through and added the canned food he had brought with him to the pantry. He was impressed to see that we had a working refrigerator that had the rabbit meat in it. Tone got us back on the road again, heading away from Evan's gas station.

He watched it disappear out the window. He looked almost sad and I wondered how he had ended up on his own in all this. I tried to think about how it would have been to be caught in the outbreak all alone. Thinking back to all the close calls we faced as a group, I knew if I had faced them without help I would be dead by now.

There was a fire burning way off in the horizon. The smoke column was black and angry looking from what I could see out the window. It made me think of Hunter's father's garage and the fire that ate away his life.

He seemed happy to have Hannah still and I wanted to ask if that meant he was closer to her. Or if it meant she was the only member of his family he had worried about. I couldn't ask him though; it would be cruel to make him talk about the loss of his family.

I looked towards where Sam had said Paradis Roulette was and I could see that the dome was looking bigger. More of it was visible which was a good sign. It meant we were closer.

Evan hadn't integrated himself into the group. He was sitting off by himself watching everyone else interact. He was staying quiet but he had a notebook in front of him that he was doing something in. I finally got curious enough to go and see what he was doing. I sat down next to him and looked at the paper in the book he was holding up with his knees. He was drawing everyone on the bus. Even with me sitting next to him, he kept working on a girl sitting by the window looking out. The girl was me, where I'd been sitting before coming over to see what he was doing.

"You're good." I told him and he smiled before putting the pencil he was using down.

"Thank you. Ashlyn right?" He responded looking at me.

"Yeah. So why are you drawing all of us?" I asked him.

"Before all this, I was an artist, now I draw what I see; keeping an image documentary reminds me that I'm not crazy." Evan answered.

"So you've drawn everything you've seen?" I asked him and he handed over his sketch book.

"Yes I have; you can have a look but I should warn you some of it is more on the gory side." He told me as I started from the beginning.

The first drawing was of a street with lots of people running and houses on fire. There were shadows going after people, but they were too far away to see clearly. The next image was of a Red Eye up close holding onto an arm that was no longer attached to a body. Followed by a picture of a little girl holding the hand of a woman in a field of sunflowers.

The next drawing showed the woman from the last picture on the ground as a Red Eye dragged her away. The little girl was holding the woman's hand, trying to pull her back. The next one was of the little girl sleeping. She had a teddy bear wrapped tightly in her arms, there were tears running down her face. There were more pictures of people sitting around a fire and then ones of them dying.

Then came a drawing of a cross in the ground, the name Eve was carved into it and a teddy bear sat by the foot of the cross. The next drawing was of the gas station overrun with Red Eyes. The next one was the perimeter he had set up, there were bodies on the ground that had arms and legs cut off. There were drawings of cars filled with people waiting at the pumps. All loaded up with whatever belongings the people had.

"Who were the little girl and the woman?" I asked him as I got back to the drawing of all of us on the bus and handed the book back.

"My wife and daughter." Evan answered as he flipped through till he got to the picture of them in the field.

"What happened?" I asked.

"Julie died saving Eve from an attack. She got dragged away while Eve screamed." Evan answered, "I barely got her out of there but there was nothing I could do for Julie." He responded.

"How old was Eve?" I asked.

"Eve was five and I lost her to the shadows. We were where I thought we would be safe, but it wasn't, they left me barely enough to bury." Evan said.

"I'm sorry." I told him looking at the drawing of the woman and child playing. They both looked so happy and carefree in the midst of all they had probably seen at that point.

"Don't be sorry, we have all lost people, being sorry almost seems like we're sorry we had them when we did." Evan said, "Miss them and love them, hold their memories near but don't be sorry."

He touched the face of the woman then the little girl.

"That's very well put." Aaron said as he sat down on the other side of me. "You've got some talent there." Evan nodded and was silent again. "I like the way you captured Ashlyn lost in her thoughts."

"She's an easy subject to draw, she stays still." Evan agreed and Aaron laughed.

"I am not that still." I told them.

"Oh Ash, you go off in your mind and a whole day could go by, and you wouldn't know." Aaron said and Evan laughed.

"Are you two related?" He asked us.

"No, actually we're not, at least not by blood." I answered, "Why?"

"You two are like brother and sister." Evan responded.

"It's more like losing people brought us together." Aaron said, "I think that forms a bond pretty much as strong as a real family's."

"I think you're right. I've been watching all of you the short time we've been driving. It's obvious you all have been through stuff together." Evan said, "Makes me glad I did come with you. It's a good reminder of the good there still is in the world."

"You're a part of that good in the world now." Aaron told him.

Evan seemed more at ease talking to Aaron and me. After hearing what he had to say about his family, I could see why he'd withdrawn himself from any group he ended up with. He watched Red Eyes tear his family apart, and who knows how many others.

I sent up a silent prayer that he had more hope being with us then he had at the gas station.

Sam finally had Tone stop so we could have lunch. Although he wanted us all to stay on the bus since we'd been seeing more Red Eye activity as we went. They left us alone since we weren't on foot. Unless they were already close and went for the movement.

Movement seemed to draw their attention until something else drew them another way.

Sam made everyone a lunch of the rabbit meat. It was a quick lunch. As soon as Tone finished, we were driving again. There was hope out there. We all knew where the dome was and being able to see it had all of us antsy to get there.

"It's been days since I had warm food." Evan was saying as he took another bite.

"Yeah, we saw your supply was canned." Hunter said to him.

"Being hungry, it didn't matter too much what I was eating but having hot food now makes me realize how much I missed it." Evan said as Sawyer came around and gathered everyone's dishes to bring back to the kitchen.

"For the most part we've been pretty lucky and haven't had to deal with the whole being on the road stuff too much. Well we're on the road but I mean like out there, since we have our moving house." Daisy said.

"Speak for yourself, they found me in a trunk of a car." Micah added in playfully, pushing Daisy.

"Why were you in a trunk?" Evan asked, looking at Micah.

"My dad locked me in our trunk when we got caught on a jammed road and got attacked by the Red Eyes. He gave me the key but the battery died in it and I couldn't get out." Micah responded. "If they hadn't driven that way and decided to clear the road I would still be in the trunk."

"That was a smart place to have you hide, do you know if your dad got away?" Evan asked.

"He never came back and there wasn't anyone alive around the area so I have to assume that he didn't but he saved me." Micah answered, "We were on our way to find my mom and sisters but I don't know if they made it anywhere safe either."

"Maybe when we get to Paradis Roulette they'll be able to help you. Maybe then you'll see if you can find out anything about what happened to your family." Evan said.

"I hope so. I don't want to think about my family being Red Eyes." Micah told him, "I hope they found a safe place and I'll be able to find them."

"Once we get to the dome, I'm sure we'll be able to sit and try to find all our loved ones. Maybe we'll be able to figure out how to go get them, if we can make contact." Sawyer said as she wrapped her arms around his waist.

"Stay like that a minute." Evan said as he reached for his sketch pad and flipped to a blank page. Sawyer and Micah both looked a little confused, but they stayed.

"He's an artist." I told them and they both smiled.

Evan had them stay like that till he had the rough outline done. I watched him fill in the lines; it was amazing to see both Micah and Sawyer start to appear on the paper. He finished pretty quick and started to do another copy of the same picture. He made a copy for both Sawyer and Micah but he kept the original in his sketch book and added their names to it.

Chapter Twenty-Two

Watching Evan draw took more time than I realized. Sam had come back to the living room and was discussing dinner.

"We're not stopping to eat dinner. I'm going to make burgers and Tone will keep driving, we are getting close to Paradis Roulette now." Sam told us as he went into the kitchen.

Sam had the last of the rabbit meat on the stove and the bus filled with smoke causing Hunter and Aaron to run around to open windows. The smoke cleared instantly leaving the smell of cooking meat. He brought out everyone's food to them on plates.

He even brought food back to the room where Sydney and Scott were still watching over Hannah. Sam ate his own food quickly. And we stopped just long enough for Sam to take over driving so Tone could eat.

The sky was starting to darken as sunset came. Sam was stretching in the front seat as he drove. The world looked to be bathed in gold as we continued to drive.

"Starting to look like we should find a place to park for the night." Tone said to Sam.

"Don't think you're going to want to pull over." Evan said from where he was sitting looking out the window.

"Why?" Sam called back.

"We got a whole horde of Red Eyes in the trees. They seem to be following the bus's movement." Evan said.

"I'm not seeing anything in the rearview mirrors, Tone go check out where he's looking." Sam responded and Tone got up to join Evan at the window.

"He's right we have definitely attracted a following." Tone called over to Sam.

"How many are following us?" Sam asked.

"A lot. It was the cooking food. We opened the windows to clear the smoke and never closed them again." Evan said, "They're following the smell of our dinner."

"Then close the windows and see if we can lose them." Sam demanded as Evan and Tone closed all the windows.

"It may help but they are following our movement now too. So even without the smell we need something else to draw their attention." Evan was saying.

"So we have to keep driving until we lose them." Sam said.

"Yeah, there are a lot of them out there and if we stop I think they could overwhelm the bus." Evan agreed.

"We need to figure out how to lose them soon. I don't want to drive at night where the headlights will draw more attention to us. We can't drive without them on once darkness comes." Sam said, sounding like he was trying to work out what to do.

"I'd suggest driving faster but with it getting dark that could prove more dangerous to us." Tone said.

"I could distract them and you guys could get away." Evan said and everyone looked at him.

"Distract them how?" Sam asked, keeping his eyes on the road.

"I'll jump off the bus and give them something to chase." Evan responded.

"I appreciate the thought, but we are not leaving anyone behind. You are staying on this bus with us and we will figure out how to get them to leave us be." Sam said in a tone that left no room for argument.

"What if we stopped long enough to put a radio on the ground? Would the noise distract them?" Daisy asked.

"Like a boom box thing?" Evan asked her.

"Yeah, use the noise to keep them from following us." Daisy responded.

"That might work." Evan said, sounding excited.

"Get the boom box Daisy, it's the only plan we have right now." Sam said.

Daisy rushed back to her room and returned with a boom box cd player.

"I found an audio book I was listening to so it'll be like someone talking." She said as she put the boom box on the dining room table.

"I'll be the one to hop off and set this up." Evan said as he took the boom box.

"We ready?" Sam called back.

"Yeah, ready when you are." Tone responded.

Sam stopped the bus.

"Go." He called back.

Evan jumped off the bus and placed the boom box on the ground hitting play. The Red Eyes were getting closer as he ran back to the door and slammed it behind him.

"All set Sam, let's get out of here." He called as soon as the door was shut.

We all gathered around the windows looking as Sam got the bus moving again.

At first it didn't look like the Red Eyes were going to stop, they were still watching the bus. Then the voice on the boom box caught their attention. They started to fight trying to get to the voice. One had the boom box in its hands and was trying to bite it.

Soon they were just dark figures behind us. The plan had worked and we were moving away from them. Sam kept driving even as it got too dark to not use the headlights. He didn't turn them on at all; he didn't want to draw attention to us. We were crawling along by the time Sam felt like we were far enough away from the horde to stop for the night.

"That was good thinking Daisy." Sam said and patted her on the head.

"Thank you but why are you patting my head? I'm not a dog." She said and started to laugh.

"Thanks for offering to sacrifice yourself Evan, but let me make this clear. As long as we can help it, we are not leaving anyone to die." Sam told Evan.

"I just thought I was newest and not really part of the family yet." Evan responded.

"You became part of this family as soon as you stepped on the bus." Sam told him, I saw Evan's eyes fill with tears; he didn't let them fall as he nodded to Sam.

"Now let's get some sleep." Tone said and laughed.

Hunter followed Daisy to her room where he had set up a bed for himself on the floor. Micah had his spot on the floor in the room with Sawyer and me. Axel gave up the bed in the room he had been using to Tone for the night while he slept on the floor.

Evan went up front with Sam and got the passenger seat all laid back to sleep in. Sam stayed in the driver's seat while Aaron plopped down on to one of the couches.

Morning came showing us most of the bio dome that Paradis Roulette was inside of. You could feel the change in everyone's attitudes. Being able to make out the bio dome and knowing we would be there soon cheered all of us. There was energy that hadn't really been there much since we started out on this journey.

Sydney and Scott even thought it would be good for Hannah to be around everyone. So they got her all set up on one of the couches. She seemed happy to be around everyone again. Although she looked pale and the wound on her arm from the bullet was looking red around the edges and swollen. Sydney was putting an ointment on it while Scott watched.

"I think it's infected, we have stuff that will help but we really need to get her to a hospital." Scott said, as Sam got the bus moving.

"There's one inside the dome." He said. "They're so far out that my nephew wanted to make sure there was a hospital, in case of emergencies. It is fully staffed."

"Perfect because the ointment doesn't seem to be clearing this at all. I can't do anything with it without clearing it out." Scott said, even as he fussed over the wound and got it wrapped again in clean bandages.

"She's going to be okay though, right?" Hunter asked, as he sat by Hannah on the couch and held her hand that wasn't being bandaged.

"I think she will be, yes." Scott answered as he finished wrapping the wound.

"You know I'm right here, you don't need to talk about me like I'm still behind closed doors." Hannah said.

"I'm not talking about you like you're not here. I'm just asking the doctor questions you can't answer." Hunter told her and she stuck her tongue out at him.

"It's good to see you back out of bed though." Daisy said to Hannah.

"Yes, the room was getting a little bit boring." Hannah said.

"It was for your own good." Sydney told her as she grabbed a pillow to put under her hurt arm.

"I know just not any fun." Hannah said and her eyes landed on Evan. "Who are you?"

"I'm Evan Smith; they picked me up from the gas station I was living in." Evan answered, smiling at her.

"Oh, well hi. See I didn't even know we picked anyone else up." She complained. "What else did I miss?"

"Only us getting stuck in the mud and almost having to abandon the bus. You know about Evan. There was last night when we couldn't stop until we distracted a horde that was following us. Which we did with a boom box." Axel chimed in as he sat by Hannah's feet.

"See all I've been doing is sleeping and out here you have been facing exciting things." Hannah went on complaining.

"Well if it helps, it wasn't fun, it was scary and if you had been out here you may have not wanted to see it all." Hunter said, seeming to be amused by his sister's complaining.

"You're probably right. I just hate that I was sleeping for so long. They kept me sedated." Hannah said, "They wouldn't even let me go use the bathroom, I had to use a bed pan."

Hunter was trying not to laugh. Hannah made it sound like she was a prisoner in the back room instead of someone who got shot.

"Must have been horrible." Hunter said, but he started laughing, losing the battle not to do so. Hannah looked at him for a moment before she started laughing too.

"I guess it was better than dad locking me up." She finally said.

"Yeah, you knew why they were keeping you in there." Axel said.

Sydney came out from the kitchen; she gave Hannah a couple of pain pills. To help her stay comfortable and hopefully help fight off the infection.

"We are going to be getting to the dome today." Sam called back from the front of the bus making everyone cheer and look out the windows.

"How long do you think till we're there?" Sydney asked him.

"Not long if the way is as clear as it looks to be, all that driving last night put us closer than I thought we were." Sam answered her.

He had a determined look on his face and it seemed we were going a bit faster than we had the last couple of days.

Sam was right that getting to the dome didn't take much longer after he had told us.

We were all watching out of the windows as the dome grew in size as we got closer. Soon, we were parked in front of the entrance that had 'Paradis Roulette' scrawled across it in gold. Sam stopped by a call box and hit a button. The rest of us were in awe of the size of the dome. There was beeping from the box before a voice came over.

"Sorry we are not open." The voice said.

"Drew?" Sam asked.

"No." The voice answered.

"Well go and get Drew, he's expecting us." Sam demanded. The voice didn't respond. I was starting to worry that we were going to be turned away after everything it took to get here.

"This is Drew." A new voice came over.

"Drew its Sam." Sam told him.

"Welcome back Uncle." Drew said as he laughed, he sounded relieved to hear his uncle had made it. "I was sure you weren't going to make it since I haven't heard from you and I thought you'd be here days ago."

"Well it's a mess out here Drew, but we do have a girl here. She's been shot and we got the bullet out but the wound is infected." Sam told him.

"I'm going to open the doors then drive straight to the hospital, I'll meet you there." Drew said. We all watched the gate out the window. I could feel my heart pounding as we waited. There was a low rumble as the gate started to open. It split in the middle like an elevator door. As soon as they were open Sam drove through and hit a button on another box past the doors. That seemed to be the signal for the doors to close. Sam stayed parked there for a minute while they slid closed; as soon as they met in the middle he started driving.

Chapter Twenty-Three

We pulled up to the hospital; there was a tall skinny guy with spiked light-brown hair waiting for us. He was standing next to a golf cart type of vehicle with a girl who had long ruby-red hair. Sam got out of the bus and greeted him with a hug. We all got off the bus slowly, not sure what to expect.

"This is Drew." Sam said. "Drew, meet everyone."

Sam introduced us all while he pointed us out.

"You guys sure packed a bunch of you on that bus and I'm guessing from the look of you all, there wasn't a shower." The red-head said, eyeing us.

"This is Diamond, my girlfriend. Please forgive her rudeness, she wouldn't know what to do being on a bus with a group for survival." Drew said and Diamond shot daggers at him with her eyes.

"Where's Denny?" Sam asked.

"He's around somewhere; I couldn't find him to tell him you were here." Drew answered. I noticed his eyes were chocolate colored as my gaze met his.

He smiled at me and I couldn't help comparing myself to Diamond, who was standing next to him, watching. Her long red hair straightened and her green eyes were lined with black eyeliner and done up with a smoky eye look. She had her lips red and she was wearing some sort of designer clothes.

I had my long brown hair in a ponytail, no make-up. I probably still had dirt on my face, and I was wearing jeans and a black tank top. Diamond was eyeing me when she saw Drew was looking at me. I shifted, uncomfortable and found Aaron.

"Looks like you're making friends." He told me, nodding towards Drew and Diamond.

"Oh yeah, maybe if looks could kill, her and I could be best friends." I responded, avoiding looking back at the couple.

"Yeah little mermaid over there is shooting daggers at you but the boy looks curious." Aaron told me.

"Little mermaid? Really?" I asked him.

"It's the hair." Aaron responded laughing as a wheelchair was brought out for Hannah.

"I hope you won't be offended but I'm going to have all of you stay in the hospital tonight. For observation and so I can get rooms ready for everyone." Drew told us, "If things are as bad as you said, I have to keep everyone here safe. We'll bring everyone clean clothes and you all can shower and relax."

I noticed Daisy looked a little nervous leaving the bus. I realized she hadn't been off the bus for any long period of time since Tone and Sydney had found her on it. Everyone else seemed excited about having some space.

We had gotten a bit crowded lately on the bus living on top of each other at all times. Sam was talking to Drew as we followed the nurse taking Hannah into the hospital. There were a couple more nurses waiting for us when we came through the doors.

"Males go with Joe. Females come with me, my name is Mary." The older nurse said to us. Aaron squeezed my hand and smiled at me.

"I'll see you soon." He said as he headed over to Joe. I realized I was shaking as we followed Mary down the corridors. The nurse pushing Hannah seemed to be heading the same way as us.

"I'm sure you're all ready for a shower and new clothes." Mary was saying, "We're going to have you use the showers in the locker room. Don't worry there's individual stalls."

They took Hannah.

The rest of us were given bags. They contained soap, shampoo, conditioner, hairbrush, toothbrush, toothpaste, sweatpants, and T-shirts. We were directed to the women's locker room and told to meet up at the nurse's station when we were done.

In the locker room there were separate stalls with showers. All four of us found a stall and after entering, found there were bags with directions. We were to put our names on the bag and place all our clothes and shoes into it, and then drop it down the chute.

The hot water felt like heaven and I was surprised to see how much dirt was coming off me. The water going down the drain was brown. I scrubbed my hair twice with shampoo before moving on to conditioner. I stayed in until the water ran clear. I finally turned off the water and grabbed a towel off a rack in the stall. I dried off to dress in the sweats and T-shirt that were provided for me.

I didn't touch my hair till I was standing in front of a mirror with a row of sinks underneath it. I brushed my teeth as soon as I had my hair brushed out. Sawyer was the first to join me, followed shortly by Sydney, then Daisy.

"I forgot how good a shower could feel." Daisy said as we finished and made our way barefoot to the nurse's station. Mary looked up as we emerged.

"I'm sure you all feel much better." She greeted, "Let's get you some proper clothes and shoes, shall we?"

We followed her to a huge room that had been set up with beds, like a dormitory. The guys were already there and dressed. On one of the beds there were bags with each of our names.

"Everything you need should be in there. We got all your sizes off the bags of clothes you dropped down the chutes." Mary explained as we opened the bags to find new clothes and shoes.

I felt a bit weird knowing someone had picked out a new bra and panties for me. More so that they matched, but I was grateful for them. Mary pointed to the bathrooms so we could change. When we came back Drew was standing with the guys waiting for us.

"I just talked to the doctors I have here. They informed me that the things they need to treat

Hannah aren't here. They were supposed to come on the shipment that was scheduled for yesterday." Drew started. "I hate to ask but I need volunteers that have been out there to go with me to a hospital in a nearby town to get supplies."

"I'll go." Sam said and stepped up.

"Me too." Hunter said.

"I'm in." Micah added.

"I'll go." Sawyer said and grabbed Micah's hand.

"Me too." I said stepping up beside Sawyer.

"And me." Aaron added, coming up behind me and putting his hands on my shoulders.

"That should be plenty. Sam, I'll have you drive, then you and Hunter will guard the van. The rest of you will go in with me." Drew said.

We all followed him out to where a large van was parked. The back was set up like an ambulance and the doors had to open one at a time.

"Why aren't we just taking the chopper?" Sam asked.

"I want to save it for an emergency. Plus, it'd be better leaving it here just in case we can't guard it and someone takes it." Drew answered.

"Good thinking." Sam agreed as he hopped into the driver's seat.

We all loaded up and were on our way. Drew had said the trip wouldn't take long and he was right. It wasn't a long drive, especially since the roads were clear. It was like no one had tried to use the roads here since the outbreak happened.

Before we knew it we were pulling up to a huge hospital. A helicopter had crashed into the sign in the front so we couldn't tell which hospital it was. It didn't matter to us since we were here on a supply run for more medicine for the dome hospital.

Drew led us into the hospital and at first it looked completely empty. We all relaxed a bit as we walked the corridors. We were all armed with knives. Aaron had a gun if we really needed it but Sam wanted us to try and avoid using it and stick with the knives. Drew had us round another corner near a surgery observation room.

"The supply closet is right around that way." Drew said as he pointed down the corridor.

"Just as long as you know where you're going and how to get out." Aaron said to Drew as we heard a crash behind us.

Aaron motioned for us all to stay put and went to look around the corner to see what the noise was. He came running back towards us as a Red Eye came around the corner.

"Go, get into that room." He called as he ran back to us.

Drew quickly opened the door to the observation room and waved us in. He didn't shut the door till Aaron came running in. Micah was looking out the window as Drew locked it. The Red Eyes were slamming themselves into the door trying to get in. Aaron was pacing around the room like a caged tiger; he suddenly stopped and looked at us.

"I know how we can get out of here." He said as he looked around the room at us.

"How?" Drew asked. He was at the back of the room by the window that looked down into the operation room.

"We let them in a couple at a time, stab them in the head, and we'll be rid of them." Aaron responded.

"What do you mean?" Drew asked.

"Okay Sawyer, open the door and try to only let one in.

"Micah, make sure she can get the door closed." Aaron directed. Sawyer opened the door and let one in that was dressed as a nurse, Micah helped her get the door closed again. The Red Eye went straight for Aaron and he waited till it was close enough. Then he placed one hand up on its chest to stop it and stabbed into its skull with his knife.

The Red Eye dropped to the ground and Aaron moved the body out of the way. "See we do this quickly and calmly in a manner we can control."

"Seems to be our best shot." I agreed and Aaron smiled at me.

"Sawyer and Micah, I want you both to handle the door and keep the groups you're letting in down to only two or three." Aaron directed and smiled encouragement at us.

He nodded at Sawyer and Micah while he got ready for what would come in. Drew and I followed suit with Aaron as Sawyer opened the door and a group of three pushed their way into the room. Aaron took care of one, while Drew got the next one, the last one wondered over to me. Aaron made it look easy, stab, remove knife, drop Red Eye.

My knife blade slid easily into the Red Eye's skull but pulling it out was harder than it looked. I got it and the Red Eye dropped to the ground. Drew patted me on the back as Aaron moved the bodies away.

Aaron nodded again and we got ready for the next group. Sawyer got the door open again and two came stumbling through. She and Micah slammed the door shut again. One went straight for Drew, while the other came at me. It was easier to pull the blade out this time; I was prepared for it wanting to stay.

"That's six down, how many more out there?" Aaron called to Micah.

"I'm counting at least ten." Micah answered as he looked out the window.

"Okay, let's keep this up, nice and easy." Aaron said to all of us.

He nodded to Sawyer and Micah again. As soon as the door opened and four Red Eyes shoved their way into the room before they could get the door closed again. The sound of the door clicking drew the one in the back towards Sawyer. Micah took care of it before she even got her knife pulled out. Aaron, Drew, and I made quick work of the other three.

We kept up the pattern of opening the door and taking out a few at a time that came in. It wasn't long before the hallway was clear. Micah counted the bodies on the ground as the last one dropped.

"Twenty-five of them." He said.

"That's a bit more than ten, if we only had six in here." Aaron told him.

"I said at least ten." Micah responded. We were all a little hyped from our victory over the Red Eyes. Drew led the way to the medical supply closet. He grabbed one of the hospital's laundry bins on the way to fill up when we got to the closet.

Once we got to the door that held all the medical supplies we found that it was locked with one of those keycard locks.

"I've got this." Drew said as he held up a card.

"Did you swipe that from a Red Eye?" Micah asked.

"Where else would I have gotten it?" Drew shot back.

"Would you just open the damn door." Aaron said as he kept his attention focused for any danger.

Drew swiped the card and the light blinked green as the door slid open.

Aaron and Micah stayed in the hallway with the keycard to guard us.

"Ashlyn, you follow me with that bin." Drew directed, "Sawyer, grab the empty bin by the door. Load it with bandages and anything that looks like it might be useful."

"Do we know what we need?" I asked as I followed him.

"Yeah, we have a shopping list." Drew answered as he waved the slip of paper in the air.

He followed his list as he went around the room; grabbing all that was on the shelf for each item. He went back around as soon as he finished his list and cleared the shelves of everything else they had on them. All the shelves were empty as we left the room. I noticed that Sawyer had even grabbed some of the doctor jackets.

"Was it necessary to follow a list if you were going to take everything?" Aaron asked.

"Had to make sure I got everything on the list first then took what we still had room for." Drew answered.

"Okay well let's get out of here. I think if we go back the way we came we might not run into any Red Eyes." Aaron said as he let Drew take the lead to get us back outside.

We were back by the observation room when a few Red Eyes rounded the corner. Aaron, Micah, and Drew easily took care of them as Sawyer and I pushed the supplies in the bins along with us.

Chapter Twenty-Four

The way stayed clear through the maze of corridors.

If it weren't for Drew, I think we would have gotten lost. It seemed like in no time we were outside again and heading towards the van. Sawyer and Micah jumped into the back so we could lift the bins up to them. They were adjusting the bins to make sure we all had room.

I was shutting the door that had to be closed first when I got grabbed from behind. I barely turned around in time to avoid a Red Eye's teeth. There were more coming, and I wasn't where the others from inside the van could see me.

"Ashlyn?" I heard Drew call; he must have seen the group of Red Eyes coming and realized I hadn't gotten the door shut.

"Here." I called back as I yanked away from the Red Eye's mouth again.

I was so focused on keeping myself from getting bit I didn't hear Drew walk up. All of a sudden the Red Eye went limp and fell to the ground. I turned only to find myself pressed against Drew and looking up into his chocolate brown eyes.

He grabbed my hand and pulled me back to the van. He practically threw me into the van like I weighed nothing before jumping in himself. He dragged the door closed behind him as Aaron slammed the other door.

"Go!" I vaguely heard Aaron call to Sam.

The van jerked forward and Drew's arm wrapped around me as I started to fall. I looked up to thank him as his lips came down onto mine and I was melting into his kiss. The world stopped around us, all I could sense was Drew. I felt like he could hear my heartbeat drumming away in my chest as he nipped my bottom lip. When he pulled back he placed his forehead on mine, we were both smiling, and he had my hand.

"Wow." He whispered and I nodded.

When I glanced around the van, I came back to reality. Micah was looking out of the back window watching the Red Eyes we were leaving behind. Sawyer was watching me like she wanted to say something. Aaron was glaring at

Drew, and then it hit me. Drew had kissed me and he was with Diamond. I felt the happy butterflies in my stomach die. I untangled my fingers from Drew's and he watched me as he came back to Earth.

The smile dropped off his face as I went and sat by Sawyer. I was determined not to cry and she grabbed my hand as soon as I sat down. Drew went to follow me but Aaron grabbed his arm. I was fighting back tears as Aaron spun Drew around.

"Leave her be. Don't screw with my sister. Just because your snotty piece of ass isn't here, it doesn't mean you can go around playing with someone else's feelings." Aaron snapped at Drew and I could feel the tears starting to fall.

Drew glanced at me and I saw him go pale.

"I'm not screwing with her. That may have not been the right moment for that kiss but I thought my heart stopped when I saw her in the arms of that Red Eye." Drew said, "I got caught up in the moment."

"You're going to tell your piece of ass or should I?" Aaron asked, still mad and he still had a hold on Drew's arm.

"Ashlyn I'm sorry, please forgive me." Drew said as he pulled away from Aaron and crouched in front of me, taking the hand Sawyer didn't have.

"Sorry for what? Kissing her? Having a girl? Or making her cry?" Aaron asked but didn't come over to where Drew was.

"I shouldn't have kissed you. That doesn't mean I haven't been thinking about it since you stepped off that bus. I know I'm with Diamond, but I've wanted out since before you came along. I'm not a guy who takes kissing someone lightly and if you let me, I will make up to you." Drew was pleading with me; it was in his eyes and in his voice.

"So are you going to tell your piece you kissed my sister?" Aaron asked.

"I don't want to hurt Diamond; I'm not mean like that but I am going to talk to her." Drew answered as he continued to look into my eyes.

"Look it happened and I don't know how I feel about all this. Do what you want with Diamond, but don't use me as your excuse to do it." I told him.

"Ashlyn, you are not an excuse." Drew said, standing up. "I will prove that."

I could feel the van stop and Aaron threw open the doors ready to be off, he seemed to need some space. I stood up and realized too late how close Drew was standing to me. His hand came around my waist to keep me from falling. I was blushing as my eyes darted away from him and instantly found Diamond's. I could see her take in what was happening. Her jaw clenched as her attention turned to the dark-haired guy standing next to her.

"Who's the kid?" Aaron asked, his tone implying something.

"My younger brother, Denver." Drew answered as he released me and gave my hand a quick squeeze.

"Oh, here I was thinking maybe she found someone else." Aaron hissed at him, his vice low.

Diamond's eyes followed me as Drew helped me down from the van like she was sizing me up. I followed Sawyer back to the dormitory since we did still have to stay there for now. Drew looked like he wanted to come and talk to me more but Diamond had a grip on his arm and was trying to get his attention.

"What was that about?" Sawyer finally asked me.

"I don't really know." I told her and she grabbed my hand nodding for Micah to go on ahead.

"Do you like him?" she asked me.

"I do, he's hot and that kiss was amazing, for a moment there everything else was gone." I told her.

"Maybe he's serious; if he's anything like Sam, then you know he's a good guy." Sawyer said. I knew she was trying to cheer me, and I hoped she was right.

I wondered if Drew was really going to break up with Diamond. Or if he was just trying to make himself sound like a better person than he was.

The dormitory looked different when we walked into it. Looked like everyone who had stayed here had been hard at work, making it look less like a room full of beds. They had arranged the beds into a closer arrangement. They had also gotten hold of a TV, a DVD player, and a whole pile of DVD's. As soon as we walked in we were greeted by everyone in a big group hug.

"Welcome back." Evan was the first one to say followed by a chorus of echoes saying the same thing.

"Hey." Micah was the only one to respond.

"Did you run into any Red Eyes?" Axel wanted to know.

"Yeah we did." Micah responded and they went off so Micah could tell him all about what had happened.

"You guys want to relax and watch a movie with us?" Sydney asked as she pointed to the TV and the pile of DVD's. Sawyer went over to check out what our options were. When she started laughing I had to go and see what she found so funny.

"What's up?" I asked her and she held up a box. It was *The Walking Dead*. I started laughing.

"We have to watch this one." She said as Sydney came over to see if we had picked anything. Sawyer held up the box and Sydney read it and looked at us.

"Really?" she asked.

"We can call it research." Sawyer said as she laughed.

"Research?" Aaron asked as he came over, Sydney handed him the box and he started to laugh, "Let's do it."

Sydney sighed but she got the TV on and started playing the first DVD. Everyone gathered around and seemed like they were excited about our choice. There was a lot of laughing and joking around as Drew walked in. He watched the screen for a while.

"You guys picked this to watch? With everything that's happened and you have gone through?" He asked.

"Yes, we call it research." Sawyer responded as Aaron glared at Drew.

"Where did you find a TV and DVDs?" I asked as I looked through the pile. There was *The Princess Bride, The Lost Boys, Arrow, Doctor Who*, as well as all the marvel movies.

"One of the nurses brought them in." Axel answered. A throat being cleared had us turning to look at Drew.

"Well, I came to see if you guys want dinner delivered here, or if you want to join us in the dining room." Drew said as he watched the show ignoring Aaron.

"Delivered." Sydney decided for all of us with no argument from anyone.

"Okay, I'll be back with food." Drew said. He smiled at me as he left the room to go and get food for us.

We were expecting Drew when Diamond walked in. She came right up to me and waited till I acknowledged her.

"I want to talk to you." She said.

"Okay," I told her and waited for her to talk.

"Can we go in the hall or something?" she asked when I didn't move.

261

"Okay." I said as I stood up and followed her into the hallway. Once we were there she just looked at me for a minute.

"Why did you have to go after my boyfriend?" she asked me.

"I didn't." I told her.

"Drew comes back from a supply run with you. Next thing I know he's telling me he thinks we should just be friends and I should move my stuff back to my own room." Diamond said.

"Look, I don't know what's going on with you two, but it is his choice and I had nothing to do with it." I told her and turned to return to watching the show, but she grabbed my arm.

"You haven't won. I will find a way to win him back." She told me and left. I was still standing in the hallway, a bit confused on what had just happened when Drew came with a huge cart of food. He smiled at me as I opened the door for him. I was surprised when he didn't leave, but parked the cart and joined us as we continued to watch *The Walking Dead*. He sat down next to me.

Chapter Twenty-Five

Aaron was the first one to go and investigate what food was on the cart. As soon as he lifted the coverings the scent of barbecued chicken drifted over to us. My mouth started to water and I went to grab a plate with Drew following me.

The cart was set up with an array of barbecued chicken. There was also grilled asparagus with butter, grilled tomatoes, mashed potatoes, and Texas toast. Drew followed me all the way down the line as we both filled our plates up.

He grabbed two bottles of water and followed me back to where we were sitting. Aaron was still glaring at Drew as he sat next to me and handed me one of the bottles he had grabbed. Sawyer winked at me while everyone just seemed curious.

"All the food is farmed here." Drew said, getting my attention as I took a bite of the chicken.

"That's cool and it makes keeping everyone fed a bit easier." I said as soon as I swallowed.

"Definitely, plus it keeps people busy. Gives everyone jobs to do and helps keep their minds off what's going on beyond the dome. I'll have to show you the farms." Drew responded.

"Diamond came to see me." I told him as the door opened and Denver walked in.

"What did she have to say?" Drew asked, sounding like he was walking on eggshells. Drew nodded to his brother as Denver went and sat next to Sam. I saw that Denver was looking at Daisy; he looked away when Hunter sat down next to her.

"Told me that you two broke up and that she was going to find a way to win you back." I told him as I tried the asparagus.

"And that would be because last time we broke up that's what happened. She kept coming around and she eventually convinced me that she had changed and we should try again." Drew responded.

"So she thinks if she just repeats what she did before, you'll want her back and go crawling to her?" I asked. A little amused that she hadn't thought of something else.

"Yeah but she never changes. She's your typical spoiled rich bitch who was raised with a silver spoon in her mouth." Drew said with venom in his voice.

"Aren't you rich?" I asked him.

"Yes I am, but it was important to my parents to raise us to work for what we had. We had money but I still had to get a job to buy my first car." Drew answered.

"Where are your parents?" I asked.

"They died in a car accident a couple of years ago; they got hit head-on by a guy who got on the freeway going the wrong way." Drew responded.

"I'm sorry." I told him, "I don't know if my parents are alive or dead right now."

"We'll find a way to find out what happened to them." Drew told me and put his arm around my shoulders and gave me a half-hug.

"So where did the idea for Paradis Roulette come from?" I asked him, wanting to talk about anything but my parents.

"I did a bunch of research for a bio dome project in school, so much so that my dad thought it would be a great idea for a resort. So we bought this place and built it from the ground up using my project as our model." He answered, sounding very proud.

"So what's so special about this place?" I asked him.

"Well the bio dome part means we get to schedule different weather and events for those seasons. Like right now we have summer weather but soon we will have monsoons." Drew answered. "We keep the farms in a separate little dome, like the hospital is. It helps keep the animals happy and the crops thriving."

"Sounds like it would cost a lot just to keep up with. Did you pay for everything by the room rates being high?" I asked.

"No we decided to go with the solar powering to keep the room rates down to the same as any other resort." Drew answered. "Lucky we decided that solar power was the right way to go. Now it means we have power without having to worry about generators. Or fuel to keep everything running."

"True." I agreed with him.

"So, now you know a little bit more about me, how about you tell me more about you?" Drew said. "How'd you grow up?"

"Never really paid attention to that, both my parents worked. They always made sure my sister and I had everything we could want. My sister was fifteen years older than me; my parents had her while they were still in high school. I was another surprise." I told him.

"Your sister died?" he asked me

"Yeah she did. She had a heart transplant and went crazed, Sam saved Sawyer and me. He had to kill her." I answered, "How were you able to stay with Denver and keep this place?"

"I was seventeen when my parents died, Denver was fourteen and I decided that I wanted to get emancipated and take care of him myself." Drew answered.

"That sounds hard." I said.

"Yeah Sam was granted guardianship over us but he supported my decision. He helped whenever things got tough." Drew responded. "Denver was difficult and we had to find our groove together over the bumps."

"I don't think I could have done it." I said.

"I almost called it quits a couple of times. Almost called social services to see if foster care would be better for him, but I couldn't do it." Drew said.

"Why couldn't you?" I asked, looking in his eyes.

"He was all I had left besides Sam. Dad raised us to stick together and I couldn't just send him away, I couldn't give up on him."

Drew said as he watched Denver explaining something to Sam with a lot of hand gestures. Sam was smiling at him and paying close attention.

"You're a good brother." I told him and earned a smile.

"Why thank you." He laughed and grabbed both our empty plates and brought them back to the cart.

When he returned to his spot he automatically put his arm back over my shoulders. I decided not to fight it and just leaned into him. It felt good to be sitting with someone as hot as him and know he was interested. It was also hard not to laugh at the expression on Aaron's face as he watched us. He had really stepped into that big brother role.

"Are you giggling?" Drew whispered to me.

"Yeah, look at Aaron's face." I told him and felt him fight back laughter.

"I noticed you didn't mention having a brother, so what is his deal?" Drew asked me.

"I was friends with his baby sister, Emily, before the world went bat shit. We found Aaron with his brother Wayne, who shot Tone, then Sydney shot him, and he died." I answered.

"Oh?" He asked.

"Not a real loss, his brother was a creep. He had two female Red Eyes all tied up so they couldn't bite or attack. He was planning to rape them, because one had turned him down while she was alive." I told him.

"Wow." Drew said.

"Yeah, so with Wayne dead Aaron had no intention of hurting us and helped with Tone's wound. We bonded over the loss of family and the fact that we had found a new one."

"You knew him through his sister, which makes sense. His brother sounds like he was a piece of work. I like that you guys are all so close, probably helped keep you all alive while you drove here." Drew said.

"Yeah for the most part we did lose a few people and gained some more as we went." I responded, "The hardest loss was this six-year-old boy who got bit."

"What happened there?" He asked.

"His sister Angela thought we were going to kill him and took off with him to save him. By the time we found them he had turned and he had killed her, there was so much blood." I told him and he wiped away a tear I hadn't realized was rolling down my cheek.

"You saw them?" Drew asked, he sounded shocked.

"Yeah, I went with Aaron to try and find them. We found an RV and when we opened the door there they were." I told him, "It was one of the worst things I have ever seen."

"He was six? How did he get bit?" Drew questioned.

"Yeah, we stopped by Ashurst Lake, and had lunch outside. He wandered away like kids do. We just didn't make it to him in time. Sam and Aaron did everything they could think of to stop the infection." I told him.

"I'm sorry you had to go through that. Although I'm not sorry that it all meant you ended up here." Drew said as he kissed my head.

"Can't say I would complain about being here." I agreed.

"Hey Drew, you going to head back with me?" Denver asked as he stood up and stretched.

"Yeah probably should." Drew agreed, "I'll see you tomorrow."

"Well you know where to find me." I told him as he kissed my hand.

Denver was saying something to Drew as they walked out the door together. Aaron came and sat by me. He didn't say anything for a while, just sat there watching the TV. After a while, I noticed he was watching me.

"What?" I asked.

"Do you really like him?" He asked me and looked like he was trying to read my expression.

"Yes I do. I know I need to get to know him but we're staying here. I think the fact that we are in a bio dome is going to make it hard to not run into him." I said and Aaron shrugged.

"I guess that's true, but if he hurts you I will show him it was a mistake." Aaron said as he patted my head and got up.

"Okay, we all had a long day let's get some sleep." Sam called out so everyone in the room could hear him. There was a chorus of yawns and agreement as we all found a bed to crawl into.

In the morning, the sunlight pouring into the window woke me. I lay in my bed for a while enjoying the way the light looked on the ceiling. Sitting up and looking around, I saw that Daisy was missing from her bed.

I decided to see if I could find her, so I got up and threw on my new shoes and a hoodie that was lying near Aaron's stuff. I headed out the door and was about to head to the nurses station when I heard Daisy yelling down the hall. I hurried and caught sight of her yelling at a nurse.

"Daisy, hey what's up?" I asked as I grabbed her arm.

"He won't let me go get my shoe." Daisy said and she was practically in tears.

"We can wait, it'll be fine, and it's just on the bus." I told her, "Let's go back to the room and we can call Drew." Daisy wasn't moving and before I could say anything else to her Diamond walked up looking mad.

"You really think you can win this?" She snapped at me.

"You know what, I can only deal with one crazy person at a time, and right now it is not your turn, Red." I snapped back as I tried to pull Daisy's arm again.

"What did you just call me?" Diamond almost screamed at me.

"One at a time... Not your turn." I repeated as I got Daisy to follow me.

"Wait, did you just call me crazy?" Daisy asked and I saw a smile crawling across her face.

"Yes, yes I did." I told her as we tried to escape Diamond by quickly entering our dormitory. We had no luck getting away from

Diamond; she followed us right into the dormitory.

"Look bitch, when I talk to you, you better pay attention." Diamond said as she grabbed my arm hard enough for me to feel her nails.

"I am not one of your servants. I do not have to listen to you, and right now I am helping someone else. So the line you are calling is currently busy, please place your call again later." I snapped at her.

"He is not yours!" Diamond screamed at me and brought her hand up like she was going to slap me.

"It doesn't sound like he's yours either." I snapped back. She didn't realize Aaron was standing behind her and he grabbed her hand as soon as it was up. She spun around like she was going to scream at him but was caught off-guard by the look in Aaron's blue-green eyes.

"You're here why?" Aaron asked her.

"I was trying to talk to Ashlyn." Diamond answered, her voice barely above a whisper.

"Didn't sound like talking to me, and she is helping Daisy right now." Aaron told her, "So why don't you leave and try again later."

Diamond turned and walked out of the room, like a dog with her tail between her legs. Aaron had scared her and she didn't know how to deal with someone like him. He was more of an alpha then she was and she was used to people doing whatever she said to them.

I couldn't help but laugh when the door closed behind her. Daisy joined me and we both ended up on the floor looking up at Aaron who was shaking his head.

"You are really making some friends here, Ash." Aaron said to me.

"You should have seen her in the hallway, she called me crazy but she completely shot the princess down." Daisy told him.

Aaron smiled as the rest of our group looked at us like we had lost our minds. Drew came in as we were still on the floor; he gave us a weird look.

"What happened here?" He asked as he parked a cart that smelled like it was holding breakfast.

"Oh, she just royally pissed off the princess." Daisy told him.

"Princess?" Drew asked and looked at Aaron for an answer.

"Your little red-head friend." Aaron explained and Drew's eyes widened.

"How did you piss off Diamond?" He asked me.

"I was busy with Daisy when she tried to talk to me, she started acting all bossy bitch on me, and I blew her off." I told him.

"Yeah, that would do it she doesn't do well with stuff like that." Drew said, "I brought breakfast for everyone."

Chapter Twenty-Six

"You know you don't have to use meal time just to come see Ashlyn." Sawyer told Drew, "But we all do appreciate the food."

She was the first one grabbing a plate and loading it up. She picked French toast, eggs, bacon, sausage, hash browns, and syrup. Daisy crawled over me before standing to grab a plate for herself.

Aaron laughed as he helped me up and then followed me over to the line for food. Evan was standing with Axel; he was laughing at whatever Axel had said to him. He looked like he was in heaven when he got to the food and saw what was there. Drew smiled at me as I walked up to him and Aaron walked around me to get his plate.

"So why did Diamond come to see you again?" He asked.

"Yeah, she was in a hurry, I didn't really catch what she wanted. I was a little busy." I told him as I picked up a plate. I grabbed two pieces of French toast and saw there were fruit toppings to add. So I grabbed strawberries and blueberries before moving on to the bacon and sausage. By the time I added syrup, my plate was almost overflowing.

"You know loading up your plate like that is unattractive, right?" Diamond asked, she had returned without me noticing and walked up to stand beside Drew.

She wrapped her arm around his waist resting her hand on his left hip that was closest to me. I could see Drew had frozen and lost his playful manner.

"What are you doing?" he asked her as he removed her hand and arm.

"Oh, don't be like that now Drew. Not after last night." Diamond practically purred at him as she gazed at him through her lashes.

"Last night?" Drew asked her. "I didn't see you last night; I was here with Ashlyn till well after midnight."

"You came to see me later. You told me I rocked your world and how much you are in love with me." She insisted as she watched me for a reaction.

"Uh no, I went straight back to my room with Denver when we left here, and I went to bed when I got there." Drew told her like he was explaining something complicated to a little kid. "Were you drinking last night?"

"I had a few glasses of wine." She told him, "You were so hot last night."

"I think you passed out and had some weird lucid dream. You may have drunk more than you realized." Drew told her as he batted her hand away from his face.

"Then how did I get this?" she asked as she pulled her hair away from her neck to reveal a hickey near the bend leading to her shoulder. "Or this?" She added.

She pulled the already low neckline of her shirt down further. Showing red marks right on the cleavage above and disappearing under her black lacy bra. They looked like someone had bit her in the heat of passion.

"Looks like you were playing with someone who likes to bite." Drew said.

"As I said, you were really hot last night." Diamond repeated.

"Diamond, think about this, when did I ever bite you?" Drew asked her and she thought about it for a minute before the color drained from her face.

"Then who came to my room last night?" Diamond asked looking like her mind was grasping for an explanation.

"Were you drunk?" Drew asked, sounding concerned.

"Yeah, but I know it was you that came over." She said again.

"Look Diamond, I don't know how you got the marks but you probably passed out and dreamed." Drew told her. "Now if you'll excuse me I would like to eat some breakfast with everyone here and show them to their rooms."

Diamond stood there staring after Drew as he grabbed a plate of food and led me to a place to sit. I felt bad for her; she really did believe that Drew had gone to her last night. She gave one last look to Drew before she hung her head and left the room.

"We get rooms?" I asked when she was gone.

"Yes, I have them set up on the floor where Denver and I live. I put Sam with Axel, Hunter with Hannah, and Tone with Sydney in two bedroom suites. Aaron, Daisy, Micah, Evan, Sawyer, and you all have one bedroom suites." Drew explained to me.

"I can't wait to see them!" I told him and he smiled as Denver came into the room. He looked like he was giddy and was smiling ear to ear.

"He looks happy." Drew said as he noticed him.

"Yeah he does." I agreed and Denver came over to sit with us. He grabbed a piece of bacon off my plate and ate it.

"Hey bro." he greeted Drew, "Sorry I'm not good with names, what was yours?"

"Ashlyn." I told him, "You seem to be having a good morning."

"Yes I am." Denver said as he turned to wave to Sam and I saw a hickey on the side of his neck. He got up and went over to Sam who was waving him over.

"Hey, does Denver have a girlfriend?" I asked Drew.

"I thought you liked me?" Drew asked as he grabbed his heart and pouted at me.

"I might, but no—he has a hickey on his neck." I laughed and Drew smiled before his eyes darkened. "What? What did I say?"

"Just thinking." He responded.

"Thinking what?" I asked worried I had offended him.

"Diamond was really convinced I went over to her room last night." He finally said.

"Yeah?" I asked.

"She was drunk and Denver looks a lot like me. What if he went to check on her and she thought it was me in her intoxicated state? I think my brother slept with her and he's the one who left the marks on her." Drew told me. "Hey Denver, come here a minute."

"What's up?" Denver asked as he came back to us.

"Did you go over to Diamond's last night after I went to bed?" Drew asked his brother.

"I wanted to check on her." Denver answered as a blush turned his cheeks pink. "She was all over me as soon as she opened the door. She kept saying she knew I would come to her, and dude she answered the door naked."

"Denver she was drunk and thought you were me. Please tell me you did not have sex with her." Drew said as he rubbed his temples with his fingers.

"She did not think I was you. She knew it was me and we didn't have sex, we made love, it was amazing. I always knew she would be my first and I can't wait to see her today. I think she loves me. She was wild last night." Denver said. "Why can't you be happy that she loves me?"

I elbowed Drew in the ribs before he could say anything else to Denver. After glaring darts at Drew, Denver got up and walked over to Sam. Drew looked at me.

"What?" Drew asked me.

"Do you really want him to know that Diamond thought it was you?" I asked him.

"He needs to know to stay away from her. Can you imagine what she will do to him when she finds out? Did he say she was his first?" Drew asked as some of what Denver had said caught up to him.

"Yes he did. Would she really do anything to Denver?" I responded.

"She's known for years that Denver has had a crush on her. She let him follow her around like a puppy but when it comes down to love she doesn't settle for puppy love." Drew told me.

I tried to think about how I would feel if I was in Diamond's shoes. I couldn't imagine how I would feel finding out I had sex with my ex's younger brother while I was drunk. Thinking it was my ex coming back to me. Denver looked so happy it was heartbreaking to know that his happiness was based on a lie.

"One thing at a time, when do we get to see our rooms?" I asked, trying to change the subject and give Denver a bit more time to believe.

"Soon as everyone's done eating." Drew said as a smile finally found its way across his face.

Word spread around the room that we were going to have our own rooms, everyone was excited. Seemed like they couldn't get their things together fast enough.

"Will we be able to stop by the bus and grab our stuff from there?" Daisy asked and I knew she wanted to bring her shoes to her new room.

"How about I show you guys to your rooms so you'll know where they are and then you can grab whatever you want." Drew answered, laughing a little at Daisy. I saw her smile and knew as soon as she knew where her room was she was going to the bus.

We followed Drew as he led us to a group of parked golf carts. He jumped into one of them, I followed him, Sawyer and Micah followed me. Sam got behind the wheel of another one and was followed by Axel, Daisy, and Evan. Tone drove the last cart with Aaron, Sydney, and Hunter went with him. Drew led our little parade of golf carts.

He was intentionally going over every speed bump fast to make Sawyer and me scream while Micah and he laughed. I heard Daisy squeal and

Axel laugh behind us, I looked back to see that Sam had followed Drew's lead. It was nice having fun like the world was still a safe place.

"These carts are awesome." Sawyer was laughing as she held on ready for the next speed bump.

Drew seemed determined to keep everyone laughing as we came up to the doors. They looked like the first ones we had to come through to get into the bio dome. It looked like there was a huge sprawling resort. Drew drove us up to the front doors that led to the check-in desk.

"All the rooms I save for family or friends are on this floor since this is where Denver and I call home." Drew told us, "So follow me and I will show you each your rooms."

There was a lot of excitement as we jumped out of our carts to follow Drew. Once we were inside, the first room Drew showed us was for Sam and Axel. The room across the hall went to Sydney and Tone. The next room went to Sawyer with Micah's right across the hall. Aaron's room was next with Evan's room across the way. Daisy was in the next room and mine was across from her. Hunter and Hannah had the last room down the hallway.

"The door there is to Denver's and my room" Drew said as he pointed across the hall.

"Where's the princess's room?" Aaron asked.

"The other side of Sydney and Tone's room, there's a door in that alcove. It's kind of hidden and has its own entrance to the spa." Drew answered.

Drew passed out keys and everyone dispersed to their rooms. Drew followed me into mine.

"Well you got your living room, kitchen and dining room here. The bedroom is through that door, as is the bathroom." Drew told me as I spun around taking in everything.

There were forest scene pictures on the walls; the main one had a waterfall. There was a forest green couch with blue pillows and a matching chair sitting in front of a huge TV. The kitchen was done in blues and greens to match the living room.

I went back to the bedroom to find a king sized bed with dark blue blankets and light blue pillows. The walls were all painted a light blue with the pictures all showing more abstract images. The bathroom was also light blue with the two floor mats dark blue and dark blue shower curtains.

"I love it!" I told Drew as I jumped into his arms for a hug. He was laughing as he kissed me.

"So you gave her the room right next to yours." Diamond said from the open doorway where she stood with her hip against the doorframe.

"It just worked out that way." Drew answered.

"Oh, I believe that it's more like you really wanted your plaything close. We both know you'll get bored and last night will repeat." Diamond said as her fingers found the bite mark on her cleavage.

"Diamond it wasn't me you had sex with, it was Denver. He went to check on you and you rocked his world." Drew snapped and realized what he had said.

"What?" Diamond asked, waiting for Drew to take back what he had just said.

"I'm sorry that's not how I should have told you. I found out Denver went to check on you and apparently with the wine you thought he was me." Drew said more calmly watching her like you would watch a cornered tiger.

"I had sex with Denny?" She asked sounding like she was about to cry, "Oh God, I'm so sorry Drew."

"I'm not the one you should be apologizing to. Denver thinks you knew it was him and that you are into him." Drew said to her. Diamond nodded but she didn't say anything as she turned and left my room.

Chapter Twenty-Seven

"Is she going to be okay?" I asked Drew once Diamond was gone.

"I'm really not sure." He answered, "I'll figure it out later. Right now let's enjoy your new room."

"Enjoy how?" I asked.

"DVD cabinet over there is stocked, let's pick one to watch." Drew said and I breathed a sigh of relief.

Drew decided he was going to pick what we watched. Since the last time he gave anyone from the bus movies to choose from, we had picked *The Walking Dead*. He sat in front of the cabinet for a while going over what his options were. He was humming to himself as he looked; I sat on the couch watching him. He was cute sitting there kind of off in his own mind as he weighed the choices of which would be the best movie to watch.

"Got one." He said.

"Which one?" I asked.

"The first rule of fight club is…" He quoted as he stood up waving *Fight Club* in his hand.

"Okay." I agreed to it and watched his whole face light up before he turned and got it set for us to watch. He grabbed the remote and plopped himself down on the couch next to me. He wrapped his arm around my shoulders as he hit play.

Aaron came to check on me and he looked a little annoyed when Drew answered the door. He came into the room and smiled at me, ignoring Drew.

"I'm going to see if I can find that brother of mine and break it to him that his wild night was not what he thought." Drew said as he waved to me and headed out of the room.

"I'll see you later." I called to him and turned to see what Aaron wanted.

"Hey there." He greeted from where he had sat himself down on the couch,

"Hey, how do you like your room?" I asked him as I sat down in the chair.

"It's nice. I slept on a real bed." Aaron said as he laughed, "It is really weird being off the bus. I feel tense waiting for the other shoe to drop."

"Yeah me too, it's just odd being safe." I said, "How messed up is the world that when you're safe it makes you feel on edge?"

"Oh you know, put a group of people on the road, trying to survive. Let them get to safety and they will keep looking over their shoulders." Aaron agreed as he shook his head even with the smile on his face. "Did you know they have a pool?"

"They do?" I asked.

"Yup and Sam says we are going swimming. So you have to find a suit and get ready." Aaron said and hugged me before he walked out of the room. The door wasn't even closed for a minute when Sawyer came hopping in.

"Did you find swimsuits in your closet?" She asked, catching me off guard.

"I thought you were Aaron coming back and no I haven't even opened the closet yet." I told her and she smiled as she grabbed my hand and dragged me to the closet. She paused only for a minute before she threw open the door. Revealing a walk-in closet that was filled with clothes. I walked in to examine what was there. Only to find that everything was in sizes I could wear.

"He got all our sizes from the hospital and did this. That's why he said the rooms had to be all set up for us." I said as I laughed and Sawyer showed me the swim suit options I had. I ended up choosing a blue and white polka dot two piece. Sawyer shut me in the closet so I could change and find a cover to wear to the pool.

"Can you believe we get to go swim and hang out by a pool?" she asked, almost jumping up and down. She was clapping her hands together like a little kid looking at a pile of presents.

"Sam has one of those bus golf carts out front, let's go." Micah called from the living room. Sawyer and I looked at each other and raced out the door to meet up with the group.

Outside Sam was sitting in the driver seat of what appeared to be a limo golf cart. I hopped in the front seat beside him since no one else had. He smiled at me and patted my hand as he put the cart in gear and we were off. Everyone was chatting to each other at once so it was hard to make out who was saying what to whom. Sam knew where he was going. I watched the buildings go by as he drove.

As we pulled up to the pool I saw that Scott was sitting next to Hannah on a couple of lounges. I went to say something to Hunter but Sam stopped me and put a finger up to his mouth telling me to keep quiet. He was smiling and I knew he had set this up this way to surprise everyone especially Hunter. Sam parked and everyone started unloading. Hunter saw Hannah and ran to her side.

It looked like they were both talking at once and she was showing him her wound. Hunter was talking to Scott as everyone greeted Hannah. Scott had decided to stay with Hannah in the hospital while she was healing; he said he felt more at home there.

"See Hunter? I told you it would be worth coming." Sam called, laughing as Drew pulled up in another cart hauling a grill with him.

"Who is ready for a pool party?" He asked as he parked.

"Drew, why haven't we seen any of the other guests?" Sam asked him as he glanced around our surroundings.

"Well they don't hang out at the hospital and near our rooms. Here, you'll probably start seeing people depending on what they're doing." Drew answered as Denver appeared from behind the grill.

"Hey guys." He greeted. It didn't seem like Drew had talked to him yet or if he did the message hadn't sunk in, and he was still all smiles. Drew shook his head at me when he caught my eye.

"You excited about swimming?" Drew asked me as Sam helped Denver roll the grill closer to the pool.

"Yes I am." I told him as he wrapped his arm around my shoulders and we walked to the pool. When we got close he pushed me in, I had a good grip on him that he wasn't expecting so he lost his balance and came with me.

"Well that didn't go as planned." Drew said as we both managed to make it back to the surface.

"I've been trained to be prepared." I told him as I laughed, he was laughing with me when he looked like a thought crossed his mind. "What?"

"Training, that is what we need." He told me.

"What do you mean?" I asked him.

"Tomorrow we should get together and start training so the next supply run we have to do, we move like a team." He explained to me as he dunked me under the water.

"How would we train for that?" I asked as I sputtered water and splashed him.

"We will get people to act like Red Eyes. Figure out who will be in our normal supply run team. Then train together so when we are out there we know what to expect from each other and how to help." Drew said. It was obvious that he was excited; he kissed me only to draw away again and kiss me again.

"Let's see what Sam thinks." I told him laughing and weak in my knees.

"After you." Drew said as he helped boost me out of the pool and followed me. We walked to Sam and he saw almost at once that Drew was practically dancing.

"Either you have to pee or you're excited." Sam told Drew as he tried not to laugh.

"I think we should get together a team that will be our supply run team. Have them train together against people pretending to be Red Eyes." Drew said, "Think about it as a team we would know and be able to predict what each other would do in a fight."

"Drew, that is brilliant." Sam told him and hugged him. "We know we will have to do supply runs for whatever comes up and that would make us as prepared as we can possibly be."

"Right? We wouldn't have to wonder where everyone was or what they were doing. We would know that everyone would be doing everything as planned. Not necessarily as for the run but in training." Drew was saying.

"That would be good. You wouldn't have to go and look for anyone since they would know where they are supposed to be. If they weren't, then they might be in trouble." Sam agreed and they went into what would be considered shop talk anywhere else. I went to find Sawyer to tell her what Drew was thinking, and about him kissing me again. She was of course with Micah.

"Hey." I said to her as I walked up and they both smiled at me.

"Hey." Sawyer greeted me.

"Drew has a plan to start training people who are going to be in the supply party. So they are more prepared for the Red Eyes." I told them.

"Where is he going to get the Red Eyes?" Micah asked.

"What?" I was trying to figure out what he meant.

"To train with." Micah responded like it was the obvious answer.

"Oh, he said we would be training with people pretending to be Red Eyes." I responded and Micah nodded.

"That is a good idea. Who's going to be in the supply team? When does training start?" Sawyer wanted to know.

"I'm not sure who is going to be on the team or when training will start." I told her, "I know Drew is talking to Sam about it and they are making a plan to start doing this."

"It makes sense to have a team practice together for real situations." Micah agreed, "We should have thought about it sooner."

"Where would we have practiced?" I asked him, "The roof of the bus as we drove down the road?"

"That's a good point. I guess we would have had to get here for us to be able to practice." He reluctantly agreed.

"Don't worry I'm sure you'll think of some other great idea that will keep us all safe." Sawyer said as she rubbed his arm and winked at me.

"I'm guessing Ashlyn told you what we came up with?" Drew asked as he walked to us.

"You really came up with it on your own, I just happened to say the word that set your thoughts in motion." I told him as he wrapped his arm around my shoulders.

"She helped. What do you guys think?" Drew responded still giving me credit when I didn't do anything.

"It sounds like a good plan, when do we start?" Micah asked, sounding like he was interested in doing it.

"First we'll get everyone together. Get seven or nine people to be part of the supply run team." Drew started.

"Why seven or nine?" Sawyer asked.

"Two people to guard whatever vehicle we take. Four to five people to go inside and two people as a backup if we feel we need more for a run or if someone isn't up for a run." Drew answered.

"That seems to be a good number. Keep the groups small enough that we can keep track of each other and learn how to work together." Micah agreed, sounding impressed.

We followed Drew as he gathered everyone else from the bus, to explain what his plan was. He gave brief descriptions to people as we gathered the group together. It was causing excitement. It felt like we had a real plan to help ensure our survival.

Chapter Twenty-Eight

"I guess we should start with who would want to be part of the supply group?" Drew asked as everyone sat down in a circle on the lounge chairs we all dragged over to sit on.

"How do you want to do that? Should we raise hands or do you have another idea?" Aaron asked.

"A raise of hands would be a good start." Drew decided after he thought about it for a minute. Around our circle hands went up. I saw Drew, Sam, Sawyer, Micah, Tone, Sydney, Hunter, Hannah, Aaron, Evan, and I raised mine. Drew counted and nodded.

"That gives us eleven I think we can work with that. Hannah I'll let you come to training to watch but until you're healed you won't go on runs. Or do anything that could hurt you." Drew said as he looked around at us.

"Who are we going to get to play Red Eyes?" Sawyer asked.

"I think first we should work together and get to know each other. We need to learn each other's strengths and weakness so we know what to work on." Micah responded.

"I like that. You're right that first we need to know what we have in the group. Then we get people to play Red Eyes. By the time we have a supply run to do; we will be working together like a well-oiled machine." Drew said and it was obvious he was excited. I could see the wheels working in his head to figure out how this would all work. It was interesting seeing his mind work. I found myself wondering if that was a look he learned from his dad whenever they faced a problem together.

Drew let us have our time at the pool relaxing and now all were chattering about training. Axel was hoping he could be a Red Eye and help us train. This started a game in the pool where he was a Red Eye and we were all swimming away from him calling him 'dead man, dead man'.

He had his eyes closed and was trying to catch us as we called out 'dead man' like playing Marco Polo. Sam tried to get Denver to come and join us but he ended up deciding to go and find something else to do. I think he wanted to try and find Diamond who we hadn't seen very much of since she found out she had slept with Denver.

There was a lot of splashing as Axel lunged at Daisy. She barely made it away, but Hunter couldn't change direction quick enough. Axel's hand barely grazed him before he lunged and grabbed Hunter. They were both laughing as Hunter took his spot in the middle of all of us. Everyone started calling to him and he started chasing us around. I noticed he seemed pretty tuned into Daisy's voice. I was betting he could have found her even if she wasn't in the pool at all.

"Foods up!" Drew called from where he was standing by the grill. He was cooking some burgers and hot dogs, along with a couple of cans of beans and corn.

"Hunter hasn't caught anyone yet." Hannah called back from the lounge chair she was sitting on watching us and laughing. Evan was sitting next to her and he had his sketchbook out. I was interested to see what he had drawn of us all in the pool. I planned to ask him after I got some food, since everyone from the pool was scattering up the sides to get to Drew and food.

"Looks like we'll have to take a break." Hunter told Hannah as he climbed out of the pool last, "What do you want to eat?"

"I can get my own food you know." Hannah said to him.

"Oh yeah, how are you going to carry a plate with that sling, smart ass?" Hunter asked her and she glared at him.

"Fine, go be the big brother and fend for your baby sister." Hannah said to him and stuck her tongue out as he turned away to get food for her.

Seeing them together made me miss Marie. I wondered what she would have thought about everything I'd been through to get here. I wondered what she would have said about Drew and if she would be telling me to go for it or to avoid him. Aaron came over and took my hand.

"They're cute together, makes me think of Emily and miss her. You miss your sister?" Aaron asked and I nodded. "Let's get food and we'll sit together."

"Mope together?" I asked.

"Yup that's the plan." He said as we got closer to the food.

"Hey you two. After we eat the supply group is coming with me to the gym and we're going to start figuring out what we need to do." Drew told us as he handed us our plates.

"Sounds good." Aaron responded.

We were sitting around the gym looking at each other, as we waited for Drew to tell us what he thought the best course of action would be for training. Drew looked like he was taking the measure of everyone. Judging who would potentially watch his back when we faced down Red Eyes. Diamond came in and sat watching, Aaron made a face when he saw her.

"I don't think princess is cut out for what we will be facing or doing." Aaron said as he nodded towards Diamond.

"I'm not here to join your stupid team, I'm here to watch." She replied.

"This really isn't like a show to watch or anything." Drew said calmly to her without looking up.

"I can be wherever I want; you have no say in that." She snapped at him.

"Believe me Diamond, if you get in the way here or cause any trouble with what we are planning to do, I will forbid you from being here." Drew told her, his voice dropped to ice and his teeth were clenched.

"Well back to business, Evan could you explain to everyone about how to mask our scent from the Red Eyes?" Sam cut in.

"I discovered that if you smell like one of them they leave you alone. They don't go after each other, or at least most of them don't." Evan answered as he glanced over at Diamond.

"How did you get their scent on you?" Drew asked him, leaning forward towards him.

"The first time was an accident. I was too tired to keep fighting and had ended up on the ground next to two of them I had killed. Another group went by and left me alone. There was one that seemed like it didn't care what it ate and chewed on one of the ones I was lying next to." Evan explained.

"You actually stayed next to dead things? Sounds more like a sick fetish to me. Where did you guys pick him up?" Diamond sneered and laughed making Evan clench his teeth.

"Look little girl, I lost my wife and daughter. I was tired of fighting and I gave up only to find out most of them would leave me alone if I smelled like one of them." Evan said through clenched teeth. He was glaring at Diamond who paled a little when she caught the look he was giving her.

"We got him at a gas station where he surrounded the perimeter with chopped up Red Eyes. It seemed to keep the area safe so people could fuel up." Micah said to Diamond and watched her expression change to disgust.

"So if we really get stuck we can cover ourselves and just keep a look out for one that still thinks we'd be tasty." Sam said.

"Sounds a little gross." Sawyer said.

"It is, but if it helps keep you alive it's bearable." Evan told her.

"We have a way to cover our scent if we have to. What about making something that's small enough to carry easily but can be thrown. Then when it hits the ground, it makes noise drawing the Red Eyes away from us?" Micah asked leaning towards Drew. They both looked like they were feeding off each other's thoughts and ideas.

"That should be something that would be fairly easy to put together." Drew agreed, "How much noise are we hoping these will make?"

"Enough that it draws away the Red Eyes. Loud enough that it'll be a signal to the rest of the group that we may need to hustle and get out of there." Micah responded.

"What if we could make a dice that when thrown would go off like those poppers only longer." Drew added on. I noticed them getting excited with this idea. They were both almost bouncing out of the seats they were in. They both had their heads down while they were thinking designs.

"I guess we know what their strength is." Aaron said as he smiled, it was amusing to watch Drew and Micah together.

"Yes we're both smart and like to make things." Micah said to Aaron and everyone laughed.

"Hey the idea they have going is a good one, so we know that if we need to figure out gadgets we've got people for that." Aaron said as he looked around at all of us.

"So now the redneck wants gadgets to play with." Drew said to Aaron and smiled.

"Yes, yes I do." Aaron answered. It was nice to see them getting along and not looking like they were going to go after each other.

"Who else has things we can use?" Sam asked, looking around the circle we had sat in, "We have thinkers and weapons people so far."

"Or has anyone trained in anything?" I asked.

"I have." Hunter said, "I'm a third degree black belt in tae kwon do."

"Good that means you get to go over basics with the rest of us." Sam said as he clapped his hands together. He seemed to think things were falling into place. When to me it just seemed like random stuff was getting brought up.

"This may be gross, but maybe we could come up with a bottled Red Eye smell we could spray on ourselves. To help cover our scents when we have to be up close and personal with the Red Eyes, it would help keep them away." Evan suggested.

"That's brilliant!" Drew told him. "Yes, it would be gross on one hand. On the other it would help keep us out of situations where we may have to gut a Red Eye just to cover our scent."

Ideas were getting shot all around the circle. Seemed like this was a brainstorming session of what we could do to keep the team safe. Things we could use when we would have to venture out of the dome. It was telling us how everyone's minds worked when faced with a problem. Drew, Micah, and Evan were going to go into a shop Drew had set up to bring the ideas we had into reality.

The rest of us were going to head back to our rooms. Diamond looked annoyed where she was sitting outside of our group on a stationary bike. I noticed she was watching Drew with longing, but she didn't approach him and he ignored her. I wondered if she had talked to

Denver at all or if she was just avoiding him and hoped he would move on. Part of me wanted to ask her but I knew even if I did she wouldn't answer me.

"How long do you think he'll be intrigued by you?" Diamond surprised me by asking, and I noticed we were the only ones left in the gym.

"What are you talking about now?" I asked her, getting annoyed with these little conversations of ours.

"Right now, you're new and different. You survived out there with zombies running around. You've got Drew's attention because he thinks you're brave and a survivor." Diamond responded, "How long do you think you can keep his attention?"

"One, we call them Red Eyes. Two I'm not playing to try and keep Drew's attention. I'm not like you where I have to pretend to be what someone wants to get them to want me." I snapped at her as I walked past her to head back to my room.

Diamond didn't say anything else to me, but I was sure she was glaring at me. I could almost feel her eyes throwing daggers at me as the door shut leaving her alone in the gym with her thoughts.

I was glad to get back to my room and have a bit of alone time. I found DVD's of TV shows in a cabinet under the TV and DVD player.

I ended up picking *Buffy the Vampire Slayer* to watch, I used to watch it all the time with Marie. It made me feel closer to her. I could almost pretend that she was making popcorn in the kitchen and complaining at me for not pausing. It hit me that I would never see her again, I missed her and I missed Carter. While we had been on the road trying to get here, I didn't let myself think about either of them too much.

Now that we made it here I kept wondering if there was anything I could have done differently. Anything that would have meant they'd be here with me. Just had all the 'What if's' going through my mind. I didn't notice I was crying or that Drew had come into my room and was now sitting with me on the couch.

"I knocked but you didn't answer and the door wasn't closed all the way so it opened a bit." He said to me as he took my hand, "Are you okay?"

"Yeah, just thinking about my sister and brother-in-law. Keep thinking about what if I did something different, would they be here now?" I told him and squeezed his hand.

"Your sister turned didn't she? From the transplant? What happened to your brother-in-law?" Dew asked all at once.

"Yes, she did. Marie bit Carter—she tried to attack Sawyer and me, but Carter grabbed her and she bit him before Sam shot her." I answered, "I feel like I should have been mad at Sam but I never was. Marie wasn't Marie anymore when she lunged at me and I watched Carter change."

"You've seen quite a bit in all this haven't you?" Drew asked as he put his arm around me.

"Not as much as other people may have, but I saw a bit." I told him.

"I'm going to get your mind off it." He said and kissed me. His lips were gentle on mine at first, searching and waiting for a response. When I kissed him back he brought his hand up to the side of my face, his thumb was slowly moving back and forth. He didn't deepen the kiss but stayed gentle. When he pulled away he rested his head on my forehead and looked into my eyes.

"What would you say if I asked you to be my girlfriend?" Drew asked me as he looked into my eyes.

"I...I..." I stuttered as he kissed me again.

"You should say yes." He told me.

"Oh yeah? Why's that?" I asked him as I considered what he was asking me.

"Then I won't be wondering if someone else is stealing kisses from you." He answered.

"Why are you asking me this now?" I asked him.

"The world is all chaos now, and we have to hold on to what we care about. We need to take the risks we may have thought through more a few weeks ago. I don't want to pass up the chance to be with you." He told me and I could feel myself smiling.

"You make a good point." I told him and he searched my face.

"Well?" He asked and I laughed.

"Yes." I told him and he kissed me. Then dragged me off the couch to dance around the living room. Dancing to the music playing in the episode of *Buffy the Vampire Slayer*.

Chapter Twenty-Nine

Drew was smiling as he held my hand and led me to the front of the resort. He wouldn't tell me where we were going, and only that he had to show me something I would love. At the front desk an older man was waiting for Drew.

"Ross, what can I help you with?" Drew asked him as we approached.

"I was out doing all the normal maintenance. When I noticed that by the front entrance there's a few of those...things." Ross told Drew as he played with his hat in his hands. "I wasn't sure what to do about them so I came to find you."

"You did right Ross. I'll get some people together and we'll take care of it." Drew said and Ross nodded and walked out the door to return to work.

"Looks like we are going to have to put that surprise on hold for a few." Drew told me and I caught the look in his eyes.

"What are you thinking?" I asked him.

"You're going to think I am crazy, but I think I have an idea." Drew responded as he led me in a new direction.

"What?" I asked him.

"Under the hospital there's a basement with big cages that are very secure. We used them for animals when they got sick or new animals as they came in. We wanted to make sure they were healthy before adding them to the farm." Drew started saying.

"Okay, what does this have to do with anything?" I asked him not quite following where he was going with this.

"We should try to catch the Red Eyes outside and lock them down there." Drew answered and I got why he was thinking I would say this was crazy.

"Why would we do that?" I asked him as we kept walking.

"It's a giant store room down there. The shelves and everything could almost be similar to what we will find in stores for supply runs. There's even an observation room we used to watch the animals that can see the whole basement." Drew was almost running; he was so excited. "We could use the Red Eyes to practice. Hannah can take notes about what everyone does from the observation room."

"Okay, I'm getting how this could work. Where are we going?" I asked as we rounded another corner almost running into Evan and Aaron.

"We need your help." Drew told them. "There are Red Eyes by the entrance. I want to catch them and put them in cages in the basement under the hospital. We can use them to practice with."

"You sure you want to do that?" Aaron asked him.

"Yes, can you think of a more realistic way to practice together and learn how the Red Eyes hunt?" Drew asked and Aaron looked at him for a minute.

"If we are going to do this, we are going to muzzle them so no one gets bit in this practice." Aaron said and Drew looked like a kid on Christmas morning. I wondered if he got this look every time an idea he had started to fall into place.

"Where do you want us to practice with them?" Evan asked.

"The basement, it was set up to be a store room. It has an observation room that we used to watch animals we had in the cages. Now we can use it as a way to practice what we may face in a real store on a supply run." Drew told him and Evan nodded.

"Okay, do you think we can do this, or do we need the others?" He asked and Drew looked at the three of us.

"I think the four of us can do this, we just have to be careful." He answered and we were off again.

Drew led us to where there was a truck parked that had a trailer on it, that looked like a giant cage. It was obvious this is what they used to cart the sick animals to the hospital. Drew hopped into the front and I followed him, both Aaron and Evan climbed into the bed of the truck.

Aaron hit the roof a couple of times when they were settled and we made our way to the front entrance. We could see the three Red Eyes as we got closer; they were right in front of the entrance. Drew pulled the truck over. He started to back up maneuvering the trailer to be as close to the entrance as he could get it.

"Now what?" Evan asked.

"That's easy. One of us stands on the back of the truck and gets the Red Eyes to come at them through the cage. Someone else will close the cage once they're in. The others watch and make sure those bastards go where they are supposed to." Aaron explained and Drew nodded.

"I think Ashlyn should be the bait to draw them in and Drew should close the cage." Evan added in. Aaron nodded his agreement and we got to work getting the gate of the cage open. We also had to pull out the ramp that was stored underneath.

Once we were all set for operation Red Eye capture, Drew used the call box to tell the entrance control person to open it up. As soon as there was a crack I started banging the cage and screaming as loud as I could. The Red Eyes didn't pay much attention to the guys who were all standing still and not making a sound.

They definitely smelled them. I could see their heads twitch towards the guys, but were distracted by me making noise. They stumbled over each other as they climbed the ramp to get to me. As soon as the third one made it all the way in Drew slammed the gate shut and locked it. He returned to the call box to tell them to shut the gate and all four of us loaded back into the truck. When the gate closed Drew put the truck in gear and headed towards the hospital.

Sam was outside and waiting for us. Along with Micah, Sawyer, Sydney, Tone, Hunter, and Hannah. They were all standing near where Drew was driving to. So I assumed they knew what we had done and where we were putting what we had captured.

Sam directed Drew while he backed the trailer up to a door that looked like it was built to fit the trailer in it. As soon as Sam had him stop, Drew got out of the truck and Sam walked up to him.

"What the hell were you thinking?" Sam asked him, sounding more like a father than an uncle.

"We were perfectly safe. Between Evan and Aaron, we got all three Red Eyes captured in one try and how did you even know what we were doing?" Drew responded.

"Diamond overheard you talking to Aaron and Evan in the hallway. She came to find me and filled me in on what you were doing." Sam told him, "You should have gotten a few more people, that move could have gone horribly wrong."

"You know what, you're right. I got caught up in my excitement and I should have thought that through more, but it is over and done with now. So how about we figure out how we get the Red Eyes off the trailer and into the cage?" Drew asked and Sam rolled his eyes as he hugged him.

"We could try it the same way we did with the animals." Sam suggested.

"What did you do with the animals?" Hannah asked as she eyed the Red Eyes.

"Someone would have to go into the cage on the inside and open the door. Inside there's a fenced path that leads from this door to the big cage. Once the Red Eyes are in there we lock them in and shut the rest of the doors, then remove the trailer." Sam said to all of us.

"I volunteer to go open the door." Hunter said as he raised his hand. "I've already been bit, so if it happens again, I may already be in danger of turning as is." Hannah looked like she wanted to say something but she kept her mouth shut.

Sam agreed to let Hunter be the one to open the door and lead the Red Eyes into their new home. He wanted the rest of us to stay outside by the truck till Drew, Hunter, and he came back out. Aaron looked at me and laughed as Evan sat down on the ground, his red hair looked like copper in the sun.

I heard the door open and saw Hunter pull down the ramp before swinging open the gate of the trailer. The Red Eyes watched him and went after him as soon as he started moving away from the door. Drew was the next one we saw as he closed the trailer gate and returned the ramp to its place before he shut the door. Not long after that Sam came walking out followed by Drew and Hunter.

"They're caged. Let's head in and take a look at our new practice area." Drew said, sounding giddy. We all followed them as they turned around and headed back into the basement. The basement was set up the way Drew had said it was. It looked like the aisles of a store, complete with the same halogen lights you'd see hanging in most stores.

"This is cool." Micah said as he looked around.

"It looks just like a small store." Sawyer added.

"This is perfect for what we were talking about. Now with having the Red Eyes we can get a real feel for what situations may be like out there on our runs." Evan said as he walked around checking out the space we had available to us.

"I just have to get muzzles on them and we are good to go." Aaron said.

"There's a box over in the corner that has a bunch of odds and ends in it, see what you can make out of them." Drew told him and Aaron headed towards the box.

"Once he rigs up muzzles we are going to practice. Hannah you are going to watch everything up there in the observation room. You can see the whole basement from up there. I want you to take notes on how everyone works and where any weak spots are." Sam said as he took charge.

"Those stairs there lead to that room?" Hannah asked and when Drew nodded she started off to get to her perch.

Aaron came back with muzzles that looked like they were used for the sick animals. He was smirking as he held them up to Drew.

"Those are some heavy duty muzzles for the animals deemed dangerous. Do you think they'll work for the Red Eyes?" Drew asked as he took one of them and examined it.

"Yes, my brother used ones like these on a couple of Red Eyes. They worked and kept us from being bit; these should be perfect for our group." Aaron answered. I noticed that he wouldn't meet anyone's eyes when he mentioned his brother.

"Let's get them on the Red Eyes. Hunter, Evan, and Aaron do you want to help me?" Drew asked. The four of them headed to the cage.

Sam had all three of the Red Eyes where they couldn't move. He had gotten their arms through the cage bars and tied them up. Drew and Evan started with one of the Red Eyes getting the muzzle on as Hunter and Aaron did the same with the next one. Once all three of them were muzzled, Sam gathered us together. Hannah was already up in the observation room.

"I want Evan, Aaron, Drew, Ashlyn, Sawyer, and Micah to go through the basement like you were in a store. Tone, Hunter, and Sydney. You three will be with me opening the cage to release the Red Eyes, we are going to be back up if they need it." Sam directed everyone and we split to do as he said.

Chapter Thirty

Aaron split off taking Sawyer with him, Drew ended up with Micah, and Evan took my arm and led me down one of the aisles. Sam whistled twice signaling, and then we could hear the cage door sliding open.

"When they start coming we keep within talking distance. No wondering away from each other." Evan told me, and it reminded me that at one point Evan had a family he tried to keep safe.

"Okay." I agreed as we started glancing at shelves. We were pretending we were pulling things off without actually touching anything. Before long one of the Red Eyes came down the aisle we were in. Evan quickly threw things in its path and the Red Eye tripped, sprawling onto the floor. I stayed close to Evan as we made our way to the end of the aisle and started back towards the cage. We heard Sawyer scream a couple aisles over, Evan changed direction as we went towards the sound. Aaron had the Red Eye pinned and Sawyer was on the ground.

"It came around the corner; she panicked and ended up tripping." Aaron said as he kept the Red Eye pinned. I helped Sawyer up and Evan went to help Aaron.

"Girls head down the aisle, Aaron shove the Red Eye backwards and we'll catch up to the girls." Evan said and Aaron nodded. I had to help Sawyer; she hurt her ankle when she tripped so her arm was around my shoulders as I helped her walk. We heard the Red Eye fall behind us and Evan came up beside us and swept Sawyer up into his arms as we kept going. We met with Micah and Drew joined us as we got to the end of the aisle the Red Eyes were following us. We led them back to the cage. As soon as we got them locked away Micah took Sawyer up to the hospital to have her ankle looked at by Scott. Sam waved Hannah down to see what notes she had taken.

"What did you see?" Sam asked her as soon as she had joined us.

"Sawyer is our weak link right now; she panicked and ended up hurt." Hannah said.

"Yeah, girl needs some work. She let her fear take control and if we would have been in a real situation we could have both been killed." Aaron said, he didn't sound angry at all.

"So we have a starting point for where we need to put some work in." Sam said, "How about the others Hannah?"

"Evan and Ashlyn stayed close together, looked like they were communicating. They wouldn't move on without the other. When the Red Eye came they acted swiftly and moved on. They responded to the scream they heard, they moved almost as one." Hannah read out of a note book, "Drew and Micah stayed where they could see each other. They used a lot of hand signals and also moved quickly when Sawyer screamed. The way they started to go ended up blocked by a Red Eye and they dealt with it by using what was available to them. They used noise to attract the Red Eye's attention elsewhere. They threw screws behind it."

"Well so far we have a real team starting to come together." Sam said.

"Do you think Sawyer is going to be able to handle situations like this? Real situations where people are depending on her." Hannah asked, "Panicking out there could put people in real danger."

"She can learn; this is just the first practice. We'll see how bad her ankle is and we will work with her and help her control her fear." Aaron responded standing up for Sawyer, "She's never faced the Red Eyes before and it just got in her head."

"I'm going to go check on Sawyer and see what Scott says about her ankle." Sam said and walked away.

"When you know, bring her and Micah and meet us at the edgeless pool." Drew told him and the rest of us just looked at him.

"Where are we going?" Evan asked him.

"There's an edgeless pool set up on the roof of the spa. It has amazing views and I think we should celebrate being alive there." Drew answered.

"I like this plan." Aaron said.

About an hour later I was walking to the spa where we decided to meet. Drew joined us a couple of minutes after I had; he had Diamond and Denver with him. Diamond looked defeated as she followed Drew.

"Hope you don't mind, but I didn't want her just moping in her room." Drew whispered in my ear and kissed me. I saw Diamond flinch when my eyes caught her watching us. Denver was standing as close to her as she would allow.

"I understand." I whispered back to Drew.

"Let's head up and enjoy being alive and together!" Drew called out so everyone could hear him. I noticed there were other faces mixed in with all of us from the bus. They must have been here in the dome before we arrived, because I didn't recognize them. We all followed Drew up the stairs that led to a beautifully set up pool. The water went all the way up to the edge of the roof. There was some sort of clear Plexiglas material, so it looked like the pool had no edges on three sides. There was a grill set up on a wooden deck with a few tables set up as well as lounge chairs.

"This is perfect." I told Drew.

"Yeah and we'll be up here when the sun sets. Wait till you see what that does to the water and how it looks with the edges the way they are." Drew said and kissed my hand. He headed over to the grill and lit it. He was throwing steaks on it as I turned to take in everyone around us that were here, alive, and safe. Denver looked like he was trying to talk to Diamond, but she wasn't listening to him, she was staring at Drew.

Micah joined us helping Sawyer who had her ankle wrapped. She was smiling as he put her down on one of the lounge chairs. He sat near her and they both waved at me. Aaron came over to me and watched them for a minute.

"Seems like we stumbled into paradise." Aaron told me.

"It would appear so." I told him. Aaron swept me up in his arms and spun a couple of times before throwing me into the pool. I screamed as I went airborne and came out of the water sputtering and coughing. Aaron jumped in after me, I saw Sam was laughing. Sydney and Tone were both sitting on the only edge the pool had with their feet in the water. I didn't even see Drew jump into the water till he emerged, as water from the splash was still falling around us. One of the people who must work for Drew was manning the grill and cooking something that smelled amazing.

"Look there." Drew said pointing to where the sky was starting to turn pink. The water at the edgeless sides was also turning pink. As the sky changed colors the pool water changed with it. Soon we were sitting in water dyed pinks, reds, and oranges. Off in the distance we saw a flare flying up into the sky.

"Do you see that?" I asked Drew as he was already moving to get out of the pool.

"Yeah, I need a map." He said. He went over to what at first glance looked like a little table but he opened it and pulled out a folded paper.

"What is this?" I asked him as he smoothed out the paper in front of us.

"A map of the area." He told me as he glanced to where we could still see the tail of the flare.

"What are you doing?" Aaron asked as he joined us.

"That flare came from around this area." Drew said pointing down to a spot on the map. Aaron, Drew, and I looked down at the map and back to where the light from the flare was disappearing.

"What do we do?" I asked.

"We're going to go and find out who shot it off and see if we can help." Drew answered as a second flare went up into the air in the same spot.

If you enjoyed this story, please consider leaving a review.

For updates on Trisha Leazier's novels:

Amazon
Goodreads
Website
Facebook
Twitter
Pinterest

Books in this series:

The Outbreak Chronicles, Book 1—Survival Ties
The Outbreak Chronicles, Book 2—Crisis Ties
The Outbreak Chronicles, Book 3—Healing Ties

About the Author

Trisha lives in Notheren Arizona with her Husband and young daughter with their two wolf hybrids and two cats. She loves all kinds of music and loves hearing new bands. She enjoys a wide varity of different books, as well as hiking and being outdoors. With each book she completes, she feels the reality of her characters moving through their journeys into the world. To contact her you can email at trisha.leazier@gmail.com or go to her Author page www.facebook.com/trisha.leazier

The Outbreak Chronicles, Book Two Crisis Ties

Drew disappeared out of the room before anyone could say anything else. I watched as Aaron stood up with Sam, followed by Hunter and Micah. The silence remained as we all waited for Drew to return and tell us what was on his mind. It seemed we were waiting forever, when he finally returned with a guy we hadn't seen yet following quickly behind him.

"Sorry for running off but I wanted someone's opinion—who's flown over this area for years—on those flares and the location." Drew explained as he grabbed the map back out and showed the new guy where he thought the flares had shot up from.

"From what I saw over at the hanger I think you're right on the location." The hazel-green-eyed guy with the shaved head said.

"Who's this?" Aaron asked as he nodded towards the guy with the map.

"This is Leo Wills; he's the helicopter pilot for Paradis." Drew answered.

"Copter seats seven people counting myself so I say a crew of 3 should go up with me and have a crew of 3 more waiting with radios in case we need help." Leo directed as he looked over us, "Drew, I assume you are coming so how about the girl there and her buddy come with us?" Leo was pointing at Aaron and me.

"Sounds good to me." Drew agreed, "Sam, Hunter, and Micah; I want you to be the crew with radios for us to call if we need help. Sam, get one of the trucks ready."

We didn't have time to say goodbye as we went after Leo, who was already on the move to the helicopter. Drew was right on his heels moving so fast both Aaron and I were almost running to keep up. Neither one of them looked back to make sure we were following. After a few sharp turns we came to a building that looked a lot like a giant garage. Leo led us right in through a door between the huge garage doors.

There was an electric green helicopter parked in the middle of the garage we found ourselves standing in. In dark blue letters 'Paradis Roulette' was scrawled across the side of the helicopter.

"How do you like my ride?" Leo asked us as he walked over and started doing some sort of walk around on the helicopter.

"No offense but I'll be happy when we land back here and are done." I told him.

"Not a flyer then, I take it?" Leo asked.

"No, not really." I answered as he opened up a door and motioned us to start boarding.

"Well don't you worry, with me in the pilot seat you will be safe as can be in the air." Leo said as he held out his hand to help me climb into the helicopter.

I climbed in with Aaron right behind me and Drew following.

"We all need to put on the helmets; they have built in mouthpieces and headphones so we will be able to talk to each other over the noise." Drew told us as he slipped on the helmet from the seat next to the pilot seat. Aaron and I mimicked what he did with a couple of the helmets that were in the seats behind Drew. Leo looked impressed when he climbed in and slipped his own helmet on. It looked like he was just flipping switches but suddenly there was all sorts of lights blinking and you could hear the propeller above us picking up speed.

"So quick question." Aaron's voice sounded in my ears.

"What's up?" Leo asked.

"How do we get out of the garage?" Aaron asked.

"Door up above us that Drew designed for this copter." Leo responded, "Now everyone buckle-up because here we go."

The helicopter started lifting off the ground and it felt like we were in an elevator until I made the mistake of looking out the window. The way the dome was designed made it so the door Drew designed to get the helicopter out of the garage opened straight into open sky. We were seeing the dome shrinking below us as we gained altitude. Drew and Leo looked like kids in a candy store while Aaron looked like he was trapped on a rollercoaster from hell. He looked at me and his eyes were wide from what I could see of them.

"How long will it take to get to the location?' Drew asked.

"Not long since we can just go in a straight line to where you think it is on that map." Leo answered as Drew pulled out his map and started to search the ground below us for signs of people in trouble. It didn't seem like much time had passed before Leo spotted something.

"Do you see that Drew?" He asked as he circled around.

"Yeah, looks like a truck that's rolled and that looks like a boat still attached to its hitch." Drew responded.